FEDERATION EARTH

Book III of the 3:33a.m series

Dana B. Auer

ISBN: 979-8-9887659-5-0

Cover design by: Jenna Zimdars-Cattani
Copy editing by: John Kimmel
Back cover photo: Gavin MCcue,
gavinmccuephotography.pixieset.com

I dedicate this last book of the trilogy series to those who lead us in our world.
As long as we continue to breathe, we write, so beware!

Dana B. Auer

"If you're tempted to tell someone the ending of a book, tell them they'll love it instead."

Dana B. Auer

ALPHA MALE

Day 430, 8:46 a.m.

Red Wing, Minnesota

"Best count shows fifteen on infrared scanners, Sir!" CPL Landers reported.

"Bring us in close enough for them to hear us, Sal." Baker opened a channel on the loudspeaker and hit the mic."

"Their posturing Sir, evasive, evasive! Their firing, RPG...." The small rocket fell to the crew's left side and, upon impact, exploded into the ground, rocking the Rover slightly over on its right side.

"They aren't interested in diplomacy!" Baker interjected to his crew. "Throw a disabling canister right into the middle of their compound so we can end this before it gets out of hand." Seconds later, a projectile discharged from the aft section of the rover's outer shell landed inside the calculated center of the group's camp and it exploded. First, a large echoing bang disorientated the group. Then a starburst explosion sent hundreds of individual smoking projectiles filled with sleeping gas into a slightly larger radius than a football field.

The people started to fall to the ground almost instantaneously. Abe couldn't believe what had just happened as this was his second experience under fire. Fear quickly turned to courage as he fulfilled his assigned duties.

"Okay, let's move in and round them all up into a containment bubble."

Baker was pleased with how efficient his crew operated.

"Corporal Morganton!"

"Yes, Sir!"

"Scan for signatures and direct us, so we don't miss anyone."

Fifteen bodies were disarmed and carried to the containment area in the center of their complex, an invisible force field bubble was activated that imprisoned the entire group. The shielding technology had been developed for protection, surrounding and securing applications.

"Time Morganton?" Baker asked.

"They should start waking up in less than ten minutes, Sir!"

Visible body movements from inside the containment field were becoming evident. They were all coming out of their manipulated dream state. The first person sat up and looked out at the Rover crew standing next to the strange-looking vehicle, she looked around, seeing all of her friends lying on the ground. The woman shook a man next to her and spoke out for him in Russian to wake up. Startled, he opened his eyes, got up to his feet, and ran directly at the Rover crew. "No, don't do...." It was too late, the invisible force field stopped the man in mid-stride and, like a rubber band, it threw him backward onto the ground. Laying on his back, he raised his head and asked this time in English. "What is this? Who the hell are you people?"

The entire group was fully awake now; some stood, and some stayed sitting on the ground.

"I'm Major Nolan Baker, of the United States Army, on what should have been a peaceful mission to help survivors." Looking directly at the man still on the ground. "Have you all forgotten whose side you're on? Are you the leader of this group?"

"No, I'm in charge!" A middle-aged man with glasses, about six feet tall, dark greying hair, and a slender build approached the edge of the barrier. He reached his finger out until it made contact with the shield, then pushed until his finger met maximum resistance. "This is new. I'm unfamiliar with this technology. My name is Alphonsa Orlov. My friends call me Al, are you guys going to be my new friends?" The man looked deeply into Baker's eyes almost hypnotically.

Major Baker recognized this type of Alpha male personality.

He felt the group was potentially dangerous and might never be fully trusted. Some of the most heinous leaders in history shared this same hypnotic trait.

"Okay, here's what I know so far. Last year two of your men fired upon a civilian couple driving a similar vehicle to ours. I am also aware that neither of those two men are with you today." Some of the group looked around at each other, silently verifying and acknowledging the incident with looks of sorrow and anger.

"Here is the second thing I know for sure. You fired on us, a weapon that could have harmed us and our equipment, without provocation. I had no other choice but to place you inside a containment bubble. Now, I don't know if I will ever be able to develop enough trust with any of you to establish a friendly, working relationship. Is this sound pretty accurate, Mr. Orlov?"

"Well, if you let us out of here, maybe we can discuss it face to face, one on one!" Al, visibly, was still very agitated being held captive against his will, and it caused the same effect on the rest of his group.

MSG Mullins voice spoke through the Majors earpiece. "Every one of them just spiked their heart rates, Sir." An evident sign of malicious intent. Trust will be nearly impossible at this point.

Major Baker decided to use Mr. Orlov's first name. "Al, I realize just how awkward all of this must be for all of you. The world simply fell apart on us, and everybody is a little bit pissed off about it, but some of us are trying really hard to get it back to some semblance of order and normalcy if that is even possible. Can I ask you all a question, please?" Baker looked around making eye contact with many in the group, his best attempt was to lead them to a point of comfort, a communication method that hopefully determines if it was a lost cause or not. "If we could all figure out a way to work together for the greater good, instead of selfishly for just ourselves, would you all be on board?" Baker paused and waited.

"Sir, only Mr. Orlov, and the wall rushers' heart rates stayed the same; the rest dropped."

"Most of you seem capable of starting over again to help rebuild the country with us. If you're one of those, could you raise your hand, please?"

"Same reading Sir!" Mullins reported. They all reluctantly raised their hands, even Al and the other man, maybe they determined that this would be the only course of action to get out of the bubble.

"We will leave you all alone so you can discuss my proposal in private. Think about staying together here in Minnesota and, with our assistance, becoming an Outpost for future growth in rebuilding again." The crew of the Rover stepped back inside and closed the cargo door.

"Sal, move us up onto that rise over there and give them the appearance of privacy. Is the microphone in place, O'Brien?"

"Yes, Sir, it's operational."

"Stay on them please and record their conversations."

"On it, Sir." O'Brien placed the headphones over his ears and began to record. The voice recorder automatically translated to English when the group talked Russian.

"Good job, team! Specialist Knox, how are you doing through all of this so far?"

"I think I'm okay, Sir!" Baker looked at MSG Mullins, and she nodded affirmation. "Anybody else hungry? This shit gives me an appetite?" Baker laughed a little, and the crew followed suit.

NO TIME

Day 444, 7:14 a.m.

Melrose, Wisconsin

Ace kissed his wife goodbye, preparing for travel to the Orlov Outpost that his new role as Governor had made necessary. Part of the new beginning.

The Rover that Elan brought to him on one of the Chinooks was the newest addition to their growing fleet of usable vehicles. Along with another dump truck, several pieces of heavy equipment that Mike liked to operate, a Freightliner semi and two fuel tankers, one was full of diesel fuel and the other gasoline.

Mike had skimmed off the top layer of ground in a large open area that became a domed garden, and then he engineered a long landing strip in another field for smaller aircraft.

Of course, no self-respecting survivalist would be without vehicles like a new Humvee and a brand new 2026 Jeep Wrangler Rubicon right off the showroom floor, a cross-section of cars they both always wanted to have since they were kids, like the neighbors 69' Dodge Charger and a 70' Plymouth Barracuda. Ace and Mike often safely destination raced when out on reconnaissance runs.

Anything new or used now was fair game. It was becoming evident; that the outpost needed some extra storage buildings.

****

Ace drove up the driveway to his old house in Galesville, deciding to stop once more, mainly for reflection, but he also had to pee.

Everything seemed the same as it was on his last visit. He noticed his vintage Pioneer stereo at rest in the living room. The turntable's clear plastic dust cover had a light film of dust on it. Antique wooden crates held his vinyl. He thought to himself, *how long has it been since I've listened to a record.*

Opening the calico hickory pantry door revealed a switch plate conveniently hidden from view which held the controls for the propane generator that powered the house in case of emergencies. When he turned it on, Ace could hear the low, dull hum from just outside the back door. The propane generator unit still worked. Ace thought it was ironic that he and Ailyn bought it for emergency use, and today was the first time he was going to use it. Nothing appeared to be lighting on fire or exploding.

A shiny black vinyl disc emerged out of the cardboard album jacket and slowly slid down onto the turntable; it was like foreplay, squirting a small amount of cleaning solution onto a polishing pad, pressing it against the vinyl, and allowing it to run in unison with the spinning record. The stylus lowering down softly, and the sound of 'No Time,' a 1970 single by 'The Guess Who,' filled the room. Red digital numbers changed from three to eight. Ace closed his eyes and enjoyed the climactic escape from reality.

STALEMATE

Day 444, 7:51 a.m.

Galesville, Wisconsin

Morning sunshine beamed through the upper windows of the broken home. Ace re-opened the pantry doors and flipped off the hidden wall switch for the propane generator. The low humming noise turned to dead silence and it became deafening.

Looking around the open concept living area left Ace with that awkward sense that he may never see his old home again.

Force of habit caused him to lock the service door before closing it behind him, letting out a heavy sigh after realizing the irony. The need to protect his former belongings was still so evident.

An old familiar sound filled the cockpit of his new Rover.

Before leaving Mike and Sue's, the two men installed a multi-disc CD player and four stereo speakers. Ace cranked up the volume as 'Candy-O' by 'The Cars' began to play.

Driving professionally was once a passion. Long days on the road in his Freightliner semi. A memory of a time when talk radio was listened to more often than music. The legend, Mike Haise on WISM early in the mornings, then podcasts of Tucker Carlson, Victor Davis Hanson, and Dan Bongino. The political division was too much for most to handle back then. Only a few million listeners a day heard the truth of what was coming. The rest succumbed to being led by mainstream media right off the cliffs, mesmerized like sheep to a bell.

All the abandoned cars and trucks that had blocked easy travel over the bridge to Winona, Minnesota were gone. Elan Must and his crew had cleared the wreckage, opening a clear route across the river.

It felt strange to be alone, traveling without Ailyn, but Ace knew his new position required caution and sacrifice. Hearing of the rover crew's experiences, he wouldn't have felt safe bringing her along to meet with this large group of new survivors.

Major Baker had expressed his concerns about whether they would ever trust them fully, and Ace certainly respected Nolan's gut feeling. Something deep inside was pulling him forward, though. Knowing this feeling wouldn't go away until he finished this task.

Alphonsa Orlov, a former U of M psychology professor, was a Russian immigrant. Family and friends accompanied him. They all had attended the University of Minnesota together on study visas. They were allowed to stay as valuable contributors to the 3M Company and other extensive manufacturing facilities near Minneapolis-St. Paul.

Ace was informed that the group lived in their small community on private acreage near Red Wing, Minnesota. Their trust and confidence in the country's state of affairs after 2016 were similar to his own. They were as uncomfortable with the federal government and the divisions politically as he was. Living in the United States, they were supposed to be free of oppressive government controls. *At least they had prepared well,* Ace thought.

He arrived at the entrance of the long gravel driveway, closed in by dried weeds and low-hanging branches that scraped against the fortified body panels of his new Rover. Ace wondered if the new SPV would have any scratches on it as the lane opened up to a large field with decayed natural prairie grass.

The driveway angled around to the right side of the hill, which left the Orlov bunker entrance collecting solar energy from the noon-day sun. A man and a woman stood up from inside a domed garden area and watched as the familiar vehicle passed, this time without altercation. Two men were standing by the front of the bunker; neither one waved nor changed in facial expression. Ace thought to himself, *we're not a glum lot* and then chortled out loud.

The Rover's cargo bay door opened, and Ace walked down the ramp, then waved to the approaching men.

"Hello, are you Dan Ayer?"

"Yes, I am," ready to shake hands but receiving none in return.

"Sorry, no one shakes hands anymore after Covid."

"Are you Alphonsa?"

"No, my name is Ivan; we'll take you to Alphonsa now."

The two men turned, motioning for Ace to follow them inside. While walking down a long cement hallway, Ace saw windows on each side. Some of the rooms had their blinds drawn, but those left open for view appeared to be living quarters.

Ace thought to himself, *no children.* That might be a question for conversation at some point.

The men pushed open two swinging doors like found in a restaurant. The room resembled a commercial kitchen. Several people were busy preparing food. The smells caused Ace's stomach to grumble.

Another set of swing doors led them to the main hall area with tables and benches on both sides. Thoughts of his grade school cafeteria, efficient but industrial.

More windows and doors lined both the right and left walls. Rooms for exercise equipment, recreation, and entertainment.

They approached a single steel door. By itself, it stood out against the gray paint. Ivan knocked twice, and a man's voice in a Russian accent answered, "come in."

Ace stepped past the two men and approached. A bearded man sat stoically behind a solid walnut desk that looked old and handcrafted. Possibly an heirloom passed down through the Orlov family tree. His best guess 16th or 17th century.

The man stood up and came around to the front of the desk. "Hello, Mr. Ayer. It is a pleasure to meet you. Can I offer you a beverage?" His tone had changed with elements of a strong English vocabulary.

Before sitting, Ace accepted a glass of water. "It's very nice to meet you, Alphonsa."

"Please, just call me Al. It will be much easier."

"Only if you call me by my nickname, it's Ace."

Al motioned for Ace to sit and made his way back around to his highback office chair. "Ace, I like that. Please share with me how you came about getting this nickname?"

Ace adjusted himself, sitting back in the chair and relaxing; he proceeded to tell Al the short story.

"That is a fantastic story Ace, so you are a great hunter then?"

"Well not always great, but I have hunted for all of my life, are you?"

"Oh yes, it has fulfilled me for most of my life too. In Russia, wild game was very plentiful. Brown bear and stag were my favorites."

Feeling like it would be to his advantage, Ace offered, "I've never taken down a bear Al, only deer for food. My wife Ailyn tried bear meat but didn't care for it, so I decided I shouldn't kill one just for the sport if we weren't going to eat it together."

Al had a puzzled look on his face. "Not every great hunter kills just for meat, Ace. Many kill for the sport—lions, tigers, and elephants in Africa."

"I never saw the point of it, I guess. I was born and raised on a farm with little means. We learned only to harvest what we could eat for food. I once shot a possum and brought it home. My Father made us eat it. I never shot another possum after that." The four men laughed.

Ace glanced over at an ornamental chessboard to the right of his chair.

Al took notice and asked. "Do you play?"

"I used to enjoy playing chess, but it's been a very long time since my last match."

"Please, let's play. We have all the time in the world, right?"

"Okay, I guess that would be alright."

The two men sat down, and Al grabbed a pawn and put his hands around his back. "Guess."

"Left"

"Ahh, yes, an excellent choice. You start first."

For the next several hours, the two men strategically battled against each other. Ivan and the other man had come and gone several times, leaving them alone to play.

Al's move, "It appears we are at a stalemate, Ace! You are a formidable player, my new friend. Only one other person has eluded me with such skill, and she went on to win a Russian title."

"You had me on the run from your very first move. I never gained an advantage. You are very skilled."

"Now I am famished. Can you eat Ace?"

"You must have heard my stomach rumbling during our game. The smells from the kitchen were making me very hungry." Again, they laughed together.

"Come, let's see what Vlad has prepared for us to enjoy."

Alphonsa offered Ace a seat and then walked around the table and sat across from him on the other side.

A second later, Ivan pushed through the swinging doors and came back holding a large stainless-steel tray of plated food; like a professional waiter, he placed the tray down on a stand and served the two men.

Ace was taken back by the beauty of the plating, worthy of a five-star restaurant. "This looks beautiful!"

"Yes, we are very fortunate to have Vladimir with us. He is a master chef. Before the chaos, he prepared meals for the executives and owners of the 3M Company. Many of our group worked for 3M."

"And you were a professor at the university?"

"Yes, psychology! What was it you did, Ace?"

"I was a professional truck driver for a concrete company in La Crosse, Wisconsin."

"Truck driver, then how does this qualify you to have a new title of Governor?"

Ace sensed the question had a hidden agenda. He paused before answering, then explained. "Al, until recently, President Baylor didn't know if I was the only man left alive in the Midwest."

"Oh, I'm sure there are many who survived and just haven't come out of hiding yet."

Feeling the need to change the subject, "Are there any children among you here?"

"No children yet, but there is one on its way." Alphonsa smiled like a proud grandfather. "Ivan's wife is due any day now!"

Ace looked over and smiled. "Congratulations, Ivan, that's inspiring news. Kids can change everything, but they are worth the effort." Ivan nodded his head and smiled like a proud father.

"The world has changed so much, Ace. Nothing will ever be the same again." Alphonsa looked down and shook his head from side to side.

"Oh, I don't know, this wonderful meal reminds me of the past, my compliments to the chef. Thank you so much for your hospitality. It's the best I've eaten in two years."

The men spent the next few hours discussing the

country's situation, and it was clear that Al wasn't entirely on board with President Baylor and Elan Must's leadership. Nonetheless, he vowed his group's cooperation on behalf of humanity and the country as a whole, no more fighting.

Ace stayed the night, sleeping in the Rover. It was similar to RV camping, but he missed Ailyn. He would go back and get her before traveling the rest of the way to the Norad Sanctuary. They shouldn't be forced apart, not by his new role as Governor, or any other reason.

Another superb meal at breakfast. Eggs, potato hash with mixed vegetables, and sweet bread. For this meal, everyone joined together in the large cafeteria hall. Ace noticed that the majority of the group chose to speak Russian. Some were talking about him; at least, that is what he sensed. Suddenly the whole experience became somehow familiar. Ace realized that he had dreamed of this very moment. He couldn't wait to get back to Ailyn to share the news.

"Safe travels, my new friend. Come back when you want to have another game of chess. I'd like a rematch!"

"Thank you for your hospitality, Al. Is there anything you would like for me to convey to President Baylor?"

"Yeah, don't screw it up!"

"Okay, I understand."

FIRST SERGEANT

Day 445

Red Wing, Minnesota

"Rover VI to NS1, do you have a copy?"

"NS1 Specialist O'Neil here, Governor Ayer, go ahead."

"Reporting in on my meeting with Alphonsa Orlov and his group."

"President Baylor isn't available at the moment. Would you like me to record your message, and I will play it back for him when he returns?"

"Yes, that sounds good. Ready when you are."

When Ace finished, he also mentioned that he would be traveling to Norad Mountain with his wife Ailyn and asked SPC. O'Neil to inform President Baylor.

"Safe travels, Governor Ayer. See you in about a week."

"Thank you, Mr. O'Neil, Rover VI over and out."

Day 445
Dallas, Texas

"Dad, you just don't understand; you never have."

"Karla, I'm your father; the last thing I'm going to do is let you leave again. You and Reese will be safer staying here with us. Why in the hell do you feel like you have to go. Look what it took for you to get here. Nolan told me what happened to you after you left Minneapolis!"

Reese stepped in, "I think your dad's right, Karla; it's not safe yet."

"What happened to all the, I'll go wherever you go Karla stuff. Look, I can't explain enough for either of you to understand, other than I have another purpose, and staying here at your ranch just isn't it, Dad. Please, can't you understand that?"

"Where are you going to go?" John asked, a little closer to surrender.

"I'm going to start at Norad Mountain and find out where I'm needed the most. I've got special skills, and I just know I have a greater purpose."

Karla walked away, and Reese followed. He knew nothing could be said to change her mind, but he'd never want to let her go alone.

John Pillsbury and Margaret watched as Karla and Reese drove down their driveway. Their feelings for Karla were as real as any could have been.

"I understand why we're doing this, Karla. It's no different than when I moved to Minneapolis, away from my parents. I needed to make it on my own, without them always stepping into my decisions."

"That's part of it, Reese, but it's more than that. I just can't explain it properly to you yet."

"It's okay; you don't have to; let's just see where it takes us, okay?"

"Yeah, I'm living on a day at a time basis. I just want to be more useful; that's what I'm sure of."

Reese settled in, with Patch lying next to them. His cloth pad was on the floor between the seats. A little less talking than on their last trip together.

"I hope these cloudy skies clear up soon. The batteries aren't charging properly."

Looking over at the gauges, Reese saw it read fifty-five percent. "Can we use the backup generator to charge the batteries?"

"Yeah, but it will only last for the rest of the day, and the propane tank will be empty too."

"Can we make it to the Cartwrights in Nevada?"

"I'm not sure?"

"A day at a time, right?"

Karla stopped before she drained the Rovers batteries completely. John Pillsbury was the last person she wanted to rely on for their rescue after leaving. They decided to camp overnight and see if the sun would reappear tomorrow. The daily convenience of looking up the coming weather on a cellphone was a thing of the past. She would call Elan tomorrow if the clouds didn't cooperate.

******

Day 447
New Mexico

"Rover V to NS1. Do you have a copy?"

"This is NS1, Specialist O'Neil. Go ahead, Rover V."

"Mr. O'Neil is Elan available; this is Karla Pillsbury."

"Hold on, Miss Pillsbury; I'll try to locate him for you."

Reese decided to take Patch outside for a short break to give Karla some privacy to concentrate on speaking with Elan Must. It wasn't raining, but the overcast skies were endless. He thought that maybe he could smell a hint of smoke in the air. Could this be remnants of previous fires from the other side of the earth caused by the annihilation of the Middle East?

"Elan, Reese and I left my parents a few days ago. There's been no sunshine since we left. Now we are a few hundred miles southeast of the Cartwright Outpost, and the batteries in our Rover are dead."

"Yeah, John called me after you left. What if I flew down in one of our cargo choppers and brought you and the Rover back to Norad? Would that be, okay?"

"I'm sorry I'm causing trouble for you, Elan, but I would appreciate that very much. I'll explain my side of all this to you when were together."

"Okay, no problem, I'm guessing that I should be there in about five hours or so. Will you and Reese be okay until then?"

"We've been through so much, Elan, and things have changed so much. Thank you for helping me again."

"See you in a little while, Karla, hang in there! NS1 over and out."

Karla stepped outside the Rover and met Reese and Patch, sitting above a dried-up creek bank. She had developed very strong feelings for him, but not as strong as the pull she was experiencing, something that she still couldn't quite put her finger on. Time would reveal it all, that she knew for sure.

"Elan is coming with a helicopter."

"Sounds good."

"I'm sorry, Reese."

"For what?"

"For the way, I've been treating you; I know I've been a selfish bitch to you by not explaining what I'm feeling."

"Karla, it's okay. The first day I met you back at the museum I felt as if I already knew you and how strong of a woman you are. I know that when you get stuck on something, nothing is going to change your mind about it. You know, that strong woman thing, like my Mom!"

Karla sat down and leaned her head on Reese's shoulder.

Her right arm was around his back. "I still love you, Reese."

"It's going to be okay, Karla!"

******

"I hear Elans helicopter!"

The Chinook landed in the open field about fifty yards away from the Rover. Sitting un-used, it had plenty of power left in its batteries to make it up the loading ramp untethered.

"Hi Karla, hi Reese!"

"Thanks for coming to rescue us, Elan." Karla greeted him with a hug.

"Here, Reese, strap these to the bumper in back. Are you guys hungry? I've got some food cubes."

"Yeah, I'll take one, please; it tastes like scalloped potatoes and ham. These things still amaze me." Reese shook his head.

"How's everything going at Norad," Karla asked.

"Well, there are a few things concerning us. We heard reliable intelligence that China has been conducting maneuvers off the Pacific coastline. We have visuals of some of their naval vessels close to our western borders inside of the demarcation lines. Naval intelligence has been working closely with the Russian Navy. Not having Space Force operational has placed us at a disadvantage. Luckily Russia is acting as our allies instead of an enemy. We can't be certain yet, but the thinking is that China is preparing to make their move militarily against us."

"Elan, I couldn't stay by my Dad's any longer. I knew something wasn't right. It felt the same way before my unit went under attack in Afghanistan. Do you understand?"

"Yeah, I think so, Karla. What about you, Reese?"

"I'm not sure what I'll be able to do to help, but I'm willing to learn."

"I heard your Mom and Dad are on their way to Norad. With these cloudy days, hopefully, I won't have to go pick them up too."

"We never told them we were leaving Texas. Can we reach

them on your radio, Elan?"

"I think so; let's give it a try. Chinook 1 to Rover VI, do you have a copy?

Recognizing the voice, Ace answered back, "hello Elan, this is Ace; what can I do for you?"

"Dad, it's Reese!"

"Hi Son, what are you doing with Elan? I thought you were still in Texas?"

"Long story Dad, but we are heading to Norad Mountain now, so I'll see you when you get there."

"Reese, it's Mom. Is everything okay?"

"Yes, we're safe, Mom. I'll see you soon."

"Okay, I love you, and I can't wait to see you."

"Love you too, Mom, bye for now." Reese turned the radio back to the original scanning frequency. "Does my dad know about China, Elan?"

"Now he does, yes. President Baylor gave him and John Pillsbury a full update yesterday. No one else knows yet, though."

It was hard to rest, but both Karla and Reese dozed off inside their Rover, the sounds of the Chinook's helicopter blades rotating above them.

A few hours later Reese awoke alone. He heard talking up near the cockpit and saw Karla was sitting in the co-pilots seat next to Elan. Their conversation ended after seeing Reese coming near. "We're almost at Norad, Reese, you better get belted in before we land," Elan suggested.

They touched down on the pad in front of the mountain's bay doors, and the Chinook was moved inside manually by a service crew. The bay doors closed and President Baylor and Maggie both waited as they all exited down the cargo ramp together.

"Hello Karla, hi Reese, good to see you both again." The President reached out both hands to greet the young couple.

"Mr. President, I'm sorry for the unplanned visit. I hope you're not upset with us."

"No, not at all, Karla. I'm glad you're here. Why don't you both get settled in, and let's meet after dinner tonight to talk about what's going on."

They followed a new assistant back to the same room they stayed in on their last visit. Patch quickly made himself at home again, refamiliarizing himself with familiar dog surroundings and smells.

******

"How are John and Margaret, Karla?"

"A little upset that I left, I'm sure."

"Can you blame them?"

"No, I understand it. Do you mind if I try to explain why I couldn't stay any longer, Sir?"

"Yes, please, maybe it will help me figure out what we are going to do with you so you can earn your keep." The President had a good sense of humor. Karla already knew her purpose.

For the rest of the week, she spent time with President Baylor and his staff. She was re-enlisted back into the military at the rank she had earned on her last tour of duty, First Sergeant Karla J. Pillsbury.

******

Day 449
Norad Mountain, Idaho

A quiet ceremony took place with only a few in attendance as witnesses. President Baylor and Maggie finally decided to get married. They announced it publicly to make it official, so they no longer needed to be secretive, hiding their true affections for each other.

"Mrs. Baylor. I promise someday we will go on an extended honeymoon together, but not until we can ensure peace for the country. Will you ever forgive me, Maggie?"

"Mr. Baylor, I'd wait until our last days together for a honeymoon, as long as I can be with you until then!"

"How did I get so lucky to deserve you?"

Maggie shrugged her shoulders and smiled.

******

Day 450

Norad Mountain, Idaho

Reese reunited with his parents, feeling that he would take less priority at this juncture of his relationship with Karla.

"Sometimes things like this happen in relationships, and none of us have any control over it."

"I know, Dad, but it still sucks. I was planning on asking her to marry me if we stayed with her parents."

"Does she know that?"

"No, I don't think so. I didn't want to stand in her way. She wasn't listening to reason and had made up her mind before I could ask her."

"Well, everything happens for a reason. None of us truly know what's to be and what's not; we just go through life doing the best we can with what we've got!"

"You sound just like Grandma Ayer. That's something I think she said to me once before."

Laughing out loud, "Yeah, she said it to me too."

Day 453

Norad Mountain, Idaho

"Sir? President Palarov has arrived. He's being escorted to his quarters and will be ready to meet with you shortly in your study."

"Thank you, General Hanifl. Let's go officially welcome him to Norad Mountain."

The official meeting brought forth demands made for Russia's assistance and protection and it came at an exceedingly large price. President Baylor wasn't sitting in a position of strength. "President Palarov, what you are proposing is not exactly what I had in mind."

"I realize this is a peculiar request. One that you weren't expecting, but what else could you offer to me and my country that properly compensates us for the losses we will suffer, both in resources and of precious lives?"

"Will the citizens who currently reside in Alaska be allowed to stay and co-exist if the state is Russian owned?"

"I wouldn't think this would be a problem if they accept the transfer of ownership freely. Of course, this may take some time and open communication between you and the current leadership in charge there."

America desperately needed the Russian Navy's assistance to continue protecting its borders against a Chinese invasion. The two appointed leaders and their attending staff negotiated a mutual contract, which provided security for land. Baylor signed the deed.

******

Day 461
Norad Mountain, Idaho

"So, I was thinking about traveling back to Wisconsin with my parents."

"That might be a good idea, Reese. It sounds like things are going to start getting a little crazy here. I heard a Chinese destroyer fired on one of General Asaeop's ships off the coast near Seattle. It might be safer to be in the Midwest right now."

"How would you feel about us stopping at the museum to collect the supplies we left behind so they don't spoil?"

"Reese, that's a great idea, yeah, by all means. Here, let me put the keys you'll need on another ring. I've been with you for so long, it will feel strange not having you in my sight."

Day 463

Norad Mountain, Idaho

"I'm not sure when I'll see you again, Reese?"

"It is what it is right?" Reese answered back, still upset that this separation was even happening.

"Reese, I'm sorry."

"You won't change your mind, right? Just promise me you'll be careful. I love you, and I want to be with you again when you're ready, okay?"

"I know, Reese. I love you too."

"I need you to know something else. Before you told your dad you were leaving their bunker, I was preparing to ask you to marry me."

"Yes!"

"Yes, what?"

"Yes, I'll marry you, but not until this is over with."
They both started to cry as they held each other tightly.

Reese walked down the long hallway, Patch at his side. Karla knew that Patch should stay with Reese.

"You ready to go, Son?"

Reese smiled at his dad and said, "she said yes, Dad!"

"You asked her? Did you hear that, Ailyn? You're going to have a daughter-in-law!"

"What? Where is she? I need to see her before we go."
Just then, Karla walked out of the cargo bay door onto the platform. Reese could tell she had been crying and still was wiping at her eyes as she approached.

"Oh my God, come here, Karla! Congratulations, do we need to stay another day? Why not just get it done now?" Ailyn was elated by the news.

"No, we're going to wait until I'm out of the Marines again."

"Are you sure?"

"Yeah, I want it to happen during peacetime and with my family." Karla's real reason was her fear of the unknown. She didn't want Reese to suffer the loss of a spouse if she didn't make it back.

"Do your parents know yet, Karla?" Dan asked.

"No, but I'll call them by radio today and let them know."

The Rover moved out of the bay doors after the mechanical platform moved into position. Karla waved goodbye as her future husband and his family ventured off the platform toward Minneapolis. She had felt her attraction to Reese from the very first time she saw him in Minneapolis.

"You gonna be okay, Reese?" Ailyn placed her hand on her son's shoulder, knowing how difficult this must be for him.

"My heart hurts, Mom." A tear rolled down his cheek as he saw the bay door close shut.

"I know, honey, I know."

******

Day 467
Minneapolis, Minnesota

Ace, could see the city's skyline in the distance. The barren farm fields changed into smaller parcels and then suburban acreage with the battered shells of homes and buildings. They neared the West Downtown area, Ace spoke out. "Wow, it's not like I remember!"

"Yeah, it'll never be that way ever again, Dad." Reese's emotions ran deep, knowing the city he considered his home for so long had fallen.

It took most of the day to work from the west side, down to the Mill.

"Remember touring the museum together when you first moved up here?"

"Go to the right, Dad, and then make your way around the back along the driveway above the river. There's a maintenance door we can park in." Reese avoided his father's continuing conversation, soon he would be re-experiencing what lies inside the museum's lobby area and it weighed heavily on his mind.

Reese got out his side door and fumbled a little to find the right colored key to unlock the overhead door. It was the white one, the same color as the door. He lifted it manually, and Dan pulled in and parked.

Dan and Ailyn hadn't experienced much of the horror of decaying bodies, as they had secluded themselves inside different sanctuaries. There was a big difference between seeing the skeletal bones of the deceased in a car as they passed compared to the museum's large open common area.

They all had masks and rubber gloves, but unfortunately, it still smelled like rotted death.

Reese asked his Mom to close her eyes, and he guided her slowly through to the hidden wall entry door. Once inside, she opened them again.

"What if we covered them all up from view, Reese? Would that help make it easier?"

"Maybe, but with what?"

"I noticed a large roll of black landscape fabric in the garage. I'll stay up here and work on covering the bodies."

"Maybe we should all just stick together, Dad," Reese suggested.

"Yeah, maybe you're right. I noticed two moving dollies out there too. It will be easier to carry the totes up with those. We can pack everything together and make it in one trip."

"How far down is the bunker, Reese?" Ailyn asked.

"Six floors!"

"Wow, that's a lot of steps."

******

Reese and his parents spent the next few hours packing what they all considered valuable and managed to get it all organized in the storage compartments of the Rover.

"Do you want to stay here for the night, Reese, or would you rather sleep in the Rover out on the road somewhere?" Ace knew from his son's countenance that the museum was causing him discomfort. It should be his choice.

"I miss Karla, Dad. Sometimes I wish we would have just stayed here together."

"It's going to be hard for a while, Reese. Let's head out. We can stop when we get out of the city and camp in the Rover tonight."

"Thanks' Dad; yeah, I'd appreciate that." Reese watched the Mill museum from the rear cargo door window getting smaller as they drove down 7th Street. He was thinking of Karla and remembering the past. *I hope she knows what she's doing*, he thought and then he closed his eyes.

PATCH

Day 468

Red Wing, Minnesota

"We're going to check in with Alphonsa Orlov's group on our way back to Mike and Sue's."

Reese experienced a quiver of unexplained anxiety rush through his body. Instead of sharing it with his parents, he kept it to himself.

The Rover turned left off the Hwy 61 state road onto a gravel driveway. Patch's head raised, and his ears lifted inside his kennel door. He stepped out of his kennel and let out a little whimper as he looked out the Rover's front window.

Ace noticed the dog's demeanor had suddenly changed. "Does this look familiar to you, Patch?" Reaching down and rubbing behind the dog's ears.

"Dad, I'm feeling uncomfortable about this. How will we deal with the fact that Karla and I killed two of their men last year? What if they can't let it go?"

"I'll handle it, Reese; I already discussed it with Mr. Orlov. He didn't justify the actions of his men. One of the men's sisters will be here, though, and I'm sure her emotions will be strong. Let's just see what happens, okay?"

Patch ran out of the door toward the men standing at the doorway. Alphonsa knelt and greeted his old companion. Patch wasted no time soaking up the warm welcome.

"Hi, Al, Ivan, hello everyone." Ace waved a greeting, remembering not to bother with formal gentleman gestures this time. "This is my wife Ailyn and my son Reese."

"It is a pleasure to meet you, Ailyn. I have enjoyed your husband's company once before. I sincerely hope you will spend some time with us all so that we can develop a lasting friendship together."

Ailyn nodded in agreement. "Yes, I hope for that too. We've all been through so much over the last two years; it's time to rebuild relationships, not tear them down."

Alphonsa spoke directly to Ace and Ailyn's son. "No truer words could be spoken. Reese, I can sense your discomfort, my young friend. I don't fully understand what transpired on that day out on the highway, but I want you to know I hold no ill will against you, and I forgive you for what that is worth. I know what I heard, and that was two familiar-sounding gunshots from one of our rifles, and then a little further down the road, I heard three more unfamiliar sounds from a different gun. When the time is right, you and I can speak of this more and fully heal together, okay?"

"Yes, sir, thank you. I'd like that very much."

"Besides, there is no possible way for you to be here with me now in good conscience if there was guilt in your heart. It takes a special man to confront the past head-on."

Patch had already sniffed the compound and marked old

spots. "I see you have taken excellent care of my Patch." It will be challenging to let him go again. Your father and I will decide who is his rightful owner through our next game of chess."

Reese looked at his dad, concerned about this turn of events. Karla certainly would object if she were here. He hoped his dad was up for this unexpected challenge. A game of skill with fifty-fifty odds; after all, Patch was originally Al's dog.

"Is Patch a purebred Al? What kind of dog is he?"

"Oh no, Patch is a mixed breed. His recorded bloodline started in 1960. He is a descendant of the famous 'Strelka,' one of the dogs sent to space on Sputnik 5. Now you can see why it is important for me to win back my special 'Patch.' Are you all hungry? Let's all go inside and see if Vladimir has made something special for lunch."

******

"Reese, place a pawn in one of your hands and put it behind your back." Reese placed the white piece into his right hand.

"Please, Al, you pick this time." Ace offered good sportsmanship.

"Okay, thank you, I'll say the right hand." Reese's body language showed he was correct as he opened both hands, exposing the white pawn.

Ace's humorous attempt at trash talk. "I'm not going to be so easy on you this time, Al." Then he laughed and began setting up his pieces.

Looking down and patting the dog's head, Al said. "Patch, you have been a good boy to me; I will play my best chess with you as the prize."

Reese already sensed what the outcome of this match would be; Patch belonged with his original master, remembering his family's strong relationship with Burr and Dock.

The two men were on the third hour of play, and it was

Al's turn, moving his bishop to take his opponent's last rook. Ace could tell that he would be in checkmate in less than four more moves, no matter which piece he moved next. Looking up at his son apologetically, he played his king over onto the chessboard and conceded the game. It was decided they will leave Patch behind.

"Excellent match Al."

"You played very well, my friend."

"Sorry, Reese, I hope Karla will understand."

"It's okay, Dad. Patch should be with his original owner anyway. What if it was Burr or Dock? You'd want them back too if it were one of them."

"Yes, that's true, son." Ace appreciated his understanding words.

Reese spent some time with Patch outside of the bunker. He noticed a woman about his age looking at him from the doorway. Was this the sister? She looked at Mr. Orlov and turned to disappear back into the sanctuary.

Al and his dad were discussing some of the current details about China's military efforts against America. Alphonsa had noticed the short interaction that just occurred, shaking his head no to the young woman.

"So, President Palarov has made alliances with Baylor? This news is very interesting to me, Ace. The price is relatively high for this allegiance, but then again, what price can you put on soldiers' lives and loss of military might."

"I'm sure Russia will take little time to establish themselves once again as a dominant world power having another viable source of earth-abundant minerals at their disposal."

"Hopefully, the two leaders can work on behalf of both countries' needs to thrive again for abundance."

"Will any of your men here be willing to act as soldiers if needed?"

"I will leave that to their personal choice, but each will know what's at stake, and we will stay abreast of the situation directly with Norad Mountain communications."

"Well, let's hope it doesn't escalate, and we can all continue as we are, working toward re-establishing the nation's growth."

The two men walked over to Reese and Ailyn. "That was one of the men's sisters you saw in the doorway, Reese. She hasn't quite fully gotten herself into a position of acceptance of what had happened to her brother. Only time will heal this wound. Maybe with my help, next time, it will be right to confront it head-on together."

"Please tell her I'm sorry it happened, Mr. Orlov. If I could go back and change it, I would." Reese didn't feel comfortable disclosing he hadn't pulled the trigger.

******

Ace, Ailyn, and Reese drove away from the Orlov bunker with a feeling of relief. All of the anxiety Reese experienced from his past altercation with this group was gone. Alphonsa made that transition simple, and the most challenging thing about the experience was losing Patch. He was not looking forward to breaking the news to Karla the next time they talked.

SURVIVOR GUILT

Day 468

Melrose, Wisconsin

The Rover pulled up and parked in front of the bunker doorway, and Ailyn waved as she exited the side door. Mike and Sue were inside their new domed garden, sowing some hybrid seeds that Elan Must had delivered on a recent trip. They all met at the back cargo doors of the Rover.

"These new supplies will come in handy, Ace!" Mike grabbed ahold of one of the clear plastic totes, turning to carry it down the hallway to the storage shelves. He passed Reese coming back out. "Where's Karla, Reese?" Mike asked.

"She stayed behind at Norad Mountain." Mike could see the young man was distressed talking about it.

"You want to give us a hand, Jake?" Mike asked.

"Yeah, okay." Jake got up from the chair next to his sleeping cot and walked to the sink to get a drink of water.

"Hi, Jake." Ace came in and set another tote down by Ailyn. She was busy unpacking and organizing the new food with Sue.

"Hey." Jake walked outside to the Rover.

"Wow, what's up with him?" Ace asked, concerned. Evident by the lack of enthusiasm and short communication, something obviously happened in his absence.

"I'm not sure exactly? He's been having some of the worst nightmares I've ever seen, waking up screaming bloody murder. One time he ran full bore into the wall and knocked himself out. Did you notice the cut on his forehead? I thought he cracked his skull open."

"Wow, have you told anybody else about it? Maybe we can get him some help from a doctor at Norad?"

"I figured I'd wait until you came back, then we could figure it all out together."

Jake walked back in and nearly dropped the tote to the ground without bending down. The canned goods hit the floor with a loud bang, and a glass jar filled with medical smalls shattered inside the tote.

Ailyn raised her voice a little, "What the hell, Jake?"

Jake made eye contact with everyone in the room and quickly turned around and rushed back outside.

Ace started to go after him, but Mike grabbed him by the shoulder and said, "Let him go; it's not gonna do any good confronting him right now."

"Wow, what's up with Jake?" Reese came in with the last tote. "He just took off in a UTV down the driveway. The driveway alarm started signaling his departure, the red-light bulb blinking red on the wall.

"He'll be back when he cools down." Mike accepted the disturbing behavior, knowing they would need to deal with it later on that day.

******

"Do you think we should go look for him." Ace asked?

"Yeah, he's been gone way longer than I thought he would be."

The two men walked into the garden dome and mentioned to Ailyn, Sue, and Reese their plans to go look for him.

"I'll go east and turn onto 167 Ace; you go the other way and take C toward West Salem. Let's meet at the parking lot at Betty's Bakery. If you find him call me on the radio."

They each jumped into the two muscle cars parked inside the pole barn. The exhaust rumbled as the big-block engines came to life. They slowly backed out the pole barn door. Dust from the gravel driveway rose and blew across the open field. It didn't take but a few seconds and both men had their favorite vehicles up to highway speeds.

Dan, wasn't sure of the amount of time that had passed since Jake left the bunker. What were the chances of them catching up to his UTV? It had been several hours at least, and depending on his chosen path of travel and speed, Jake could already be in La Crosse by now.

"Mike, you got a copy?"

"Yeah, go ahead, Ace." Both vehicles had CB radios to communicate together with.

"Hey, I think I found some of Jake's tire tracks on the intersection turning onto Highway C. Maybe you should cut back over to me. I'll wait for you where Alder Road crosses the highway. We can drive together in the Charger and make better time now that we know which direction he went."

"Okay, I'll be right there."

Ace had his driver-side window down, and he had parked safely off to the side of the road. He could hear the sound of the Charger's headers and dual exhaust getting louder. Mike had a long straight-away before he arrived at the intersection.

Ace smiled, knowing that Mike had opened up both four-barrel carburetors and then shortly after heard the smooth deceleration and downshifting as he slowed down and stopped next to the classic Plymouth.

Ace rolled up his window, pulled the keys, and then locked the doors, practicing this sense of security for most of his life, unlike his peers. He knew that no one would ever find the car because no one was alive to touch it, but he just couldn't let himself leave the vehicle unlocked.

"Okay, buddy, let's see if we can go find him."

"Where do you think he's going?"

"I'm not sure; maybe he's heading back to where Pete and Beamer died?"

"Really?" Why?"

"I don't know, survivor guilt maybe?"

"Jake never told us exactly where it happened. Did he tell you?"

"Shit! No, I don't think he ever did? Maybe we can catch up to him in West Salem?"

"Okay, strap yourself in, bud. I'm going to push it a little."

Ace buckled his seat belt as Mike began to powershift from first to second. The sixty-inch tires bit and the G-force pushed them back into the seats.

"How's he been while I've been gone, Mike?"

"Kind of withdrawn. It got worse each day. I kept offering to talk about it with him, but he refused and started spending more time isolating himself from me. I think I heard him crying once a few nights ago."

"No shit? You said his nightmares were pretty intense?"

"Yeah, a few times I yelled for him to wake up. It was two nights ago when he ran into the wall."

"Hopefully, we can find him, Mike, and try and get him some help. It doesn't sound like he's in his right mind."

******

They searched the roads in West Salem until dark and lost all sign of Jake's direction. It was like looking for a lost pet with no help from the locals.

PAY BACK'S A BITCH

Day 468

Norad Mountain, Idaho

Specialist O'Neil reports, "Sir, we just received a transmission from Admiral Asaeop that China has landed approximately four thousand soldiers onto the new coastline just inside Arizona's western border. They are establishing a defendable perimeter with anti-aircraft and short-range missile capabilities."

"General Hanifl, your thoughts please?" The President was a capable military strategist, but his cabinet's credentials better served his trust and confidence.

"Mr. President, I have the Arizona 158th Maneuver Enhancement Brigade and their Infantry Battalion standing by awaiting orders for advancement. Approximately three thousand soldiers have established a line of defense, and half of the 285th Assault Helicopter Battalion and the 98th Aviation Troop Commands currently are dispersed between three Arizona airfields. Also, Seal Team Reconnaissance and Sniper teams are in elevated positions surrounding the enemies' perimeter."

"Thank you, General; what about Russian support?"

"The Russian Navy has secured waters north of the Chinese fleet, and the Armada de Mexico Naval fleet protects its coastline from further assault. They are squeezing the Chinese Liberation Forces into a funnel, which does provide us a slight advantage militarily, but China's Maritime destructive capabilities are technically unmatched. They developed advanced long and short-range weapon superiority with little to no resistance or competition between 2020 to 2024."

"I understand the Canadian Armed Forces have taken a position protecting their borders along with cooperation from President Palarov's ground forces. It appears we have our enemy's outnumbered and at a slight disadvantage, General?"

"Yes, Sir, but we shouldn't underestimate China's resolve. Our country has already suffered one nuclear hit, Sir. The only card we have to prevent them from using nuclear weapons on us is that we have two of our atomic submarines currently maneuvering just outside of China's homeland. Their only option now is to escalate a ground force attack while facing the realization of the potential destruction of their home continent."

"Are we beyond diplomatic conversation, General?"

"Yes, Sir, right after they fired upon the U.S.S Kingman. Their intentions became evident, Sir."

"Okay, I'll sign a drafted declaration of war. Do everything in your power to prevent casualties, and let's work toward pushing them out to sea back into International waters and off of U.S. soil."

******

General Hanifl led the coalition of forces advancing against the Chinese military. After the first strike, the land forces suffered severe casualties from short-range missile attacks. The Russian and Mexican Naval fleets managed to shut off the supply chain to the land-based forces. Several National Guard troops from Texas, New Mexico, Oklahoma, and Missouri, were called in to assist.

The fighting went on for days, with strategic hits to both sides of the effort. China made a final push forward, landing more ground forces like a wedge that pushed about a hundred miles inland toward Phoenix, then spreading out in both directions again like the shape of an hourglass.

Strategists determined that this effective strategy would prove indefensible if continued across the southern border. It led President Baylor to make a difficult decision. He called for First Sergeant, Karla Pillsbury's immediate assistance back to Norad Mountain from off the frontlines.

Upon her arrival, Karla saluted the President and was escorted privately to a secure meeting area with only him and Elan Must in attendance.

"I'm sure you are wondering why I've called you here alone with us, Karla?"

"Yes, Sir, it seems a bit peculiar, Sir."

"I'll get right to the point then. Chinese forces have discovered a chink in our forces along the southern border. If not stopped soon, we may all find ourselves, prisoners of war, under the control of the CCP. What I have to share with you can't leave this room, Karla, am I clear? You're the only person I trust to follow through with my plan."

"Yes, Sir!"

"A team of scientists during the Mrung administration developed a viral agent through gain of function research that will only attach itself to persons of Asian decent."

"President Baylor, are you suggesting some kind of bacterial warfare? That would go against every treaty and declaration ever signed by the world's governments."

"I know it does. Do you remember what it was like after Covid, Karla? How everything in the world had changed, over six million people died? Elan and I know that China worked with a cabal of American political leaders to unleash that virus over the earth. They are responsible for all those lives lost. Pay back's a bitch!"

"What about all of the Asian American citizens who would be affected?"

"We have an antidote!"

Karla thought for a second before answering the President. "Okay, what do I have to do, Sir?"

POTENT ELIXIR

(August 8th, 2012, 3:33 p.m.)

Baghlan, Afghanistan

"Doughboy 1, to Scabbard 1, come in, Scabbard 1, over." An enemy sniper on top of a building just down from the long block of courtyard houses had a tactical advantage. First Sergeant Karla Pillsbury and her squad were pinned down and were taking on small arms fire.

"Talk to me, Doughboy1; this is Scabbard 1, over."

"We are pinned down and need a PAA (Position Areas for Artillery), at 36.7' 58" N, 68.42' 0" E, Scabbard1, please confirm, over."

"36.7' 58" N, 68.42' 0 " E, confirmed, over."

"Okay, keep your heads down, everybody; incoming!"

The room suddenly got brighter as the Howitzer missiles obliterated the building at the called-in coordinates.

"Doughboy1 to Scabbard 1, Good hit Scabbard 1, Doughboy out." Karla confirmed the target was destroyed. "Let's move!" Dust billowed from across the street into the room as each member of the Doughboy team exited the lower level of the building. First Sergeant Pillsbury led her team forward.

Dismembered body parts were scattered about on the ground. Evident then, their route to the extraction site should be clear and safer to traverse.

"The Scout and Sierra extraction teams should be right around this corner, Ma'am," Corporal Sanborn whispered as they approached nearer to their coordinated rendezvous point.

Just then, a single round, fired from a window on the second floor of another building above them hit Sanborn in the neck. He fell to the ground. Everyone opened fire, directing a volley of rounds into the open windows. Two members of Pillsbury's squad dragged the injured man to a safer location and began administering first aid. Blood soaked the white gauze bandages, he would need special medical attention, more than they could accomplish in the field.

"Delton, Meyer, come with me. Let's make sure that shooter is immobilized." Karla led the men into the lower entrance of the battle-scarred building. Sounds of movement up the stairs on the second floor caused them to freeze and silently coordinate their effort. One would stay below to cover the exit while the other two soldiers worked to clear the building. They extended up the flight of stairs and separated directions at the top. Stealth movement with guns set to full auto.

Karla noticed one set of footprints in the disturbed dust leading away from the hallway she had just entered. They were small and not the usual shape left behind by a full-grown man. Suddenly a door flew open, and a single shot rang out. Karla went down to one knee and opened fire with two quick bursts.

Meyer rushed toward Karla and called out to his team leader. "You okay, Sarge?"

Karla looked up at the question and nodded. No more than twelve, a young girl lying dead on the floor. It was clear to Corporal Meyer that his First Sergeant was in emotional turmoil. This type of enemy was not the kind they should be fighting.

"Come on, Sarge, let's get out of here. The EVAC teams are waiting. Let's go, Sarge."

Karla snapped out of her trance. A tear had run down her cheek, and she wiped it away with her arm. They just left her there. No one was available to properly attend to the young girl's body or give her a formal burial. The thought of it would provide anyone with an endless lifetime of anguish and remorse.

******

Later that evening, What remained of Karla's squad was safe behind their base's encampment walls. Below ground, inside a sunken bunker, they drank together. Alcohol that the soldiers had gotten their hands on, a few bottles, despite the ban placed on it by the U.S. military. The loss of Sanborn from their team was enough reason for escape. Karla was on a new mission though, to erase a whole new memory of killing a child. Though it occurred in the line of duty, knowing she was an enemy combatant, it didn't matter, she was someone's little girl whose parents would never find her again—missing in action— why was she even involved in this fight? The alcohol temporarily whitewashed the experience from her mind, which was the intended goal. It was not the first time Karla had used alcohol as a potent elixir to remedy the past, nor would it be the last. At least not yet.

******

(June 27th, 2016, 13:33 p.m.)

"Well, Pillsbury, you've been here for twenty-eight days

and have made great progress. I think you're ready to graduate from your treatment plan. How do you feel about everything?"

"A day at a time, Sir!" she said back. "Will I be able to rejoin my unit, or are my military days over, now that I'm a marked woman?"

"Personally, Karla. I think you would be able to do anything you put your mind to, I have someone I'd like for you to meet."

"Okay."

They walked together down a stairway to the basement floor of the treatment hospital. When the door to the mechanical room was opened, Karla saw two chairs, an elderly man in a black suit sat with his back to the door. She thought his shape and hair style looked familiar from behind and then he turned his face to greet her with a smile.

******

(July 3rd, 2016, 10:34 a.m.)

Karla walked up the driveway, eager to start her new secret mission. Cottonwood trees shaded both sides of the driveway. She had previously decided not to announce her arrival so there wouldn't be any fuss about a coming home party. Choosing not to drink would be hard enough without explaining to everyone why she wasn't. That part wouldn't be an act.

Punching the numbered code she had memorized on the keypad opened the door of the underground bunker entrance. An excited audible voice projected out of a wall speaker next to a security camera. "Karla is that you? John Pillsbury was very excited to see her. It had been several years since they had served together. "We're on the sixth floor."

Karla hit the button with the number six on it. The elevator door closed and a few seconds later re-opened, with all three of her new family members waiting at the entrance. The reunion became joyous, even tears flowed as they held onto each other. Karla's new mom and dad and younger brother could see a new, unfamiliar look in her eyes. That type of look from seeing things no one should ever have to see, but now it's too late.

John asked her first. "So, tell us what happened?"

"I had a chance for a medical discharge, but then I chose you three instead."

"Oh my, you weren't shot, were you?" Asked with worry only a mother or an actress could possess.

"No. It wasn't anything like that." Karla had rehearsed scenarios in her mind of how she would share the news with this new family, but now that the time was at hand, she couldn't bring the words out of her mind, so she just let it fly, adlib. "Mom, Dad, Zach, I developed a problem with alcohol. I'm an alcoholic. I've been in a V.A. Treatment facility since Memorial Day. Once I started drinking, I couldn't stop, and it finally put me over the edge, so I sought help, and now I'm choosing not to drink anymore, one day at a time."

"Wow, I don't know what to say exactly." John stepped away and placed his fingers on his chin to find the right words. "Did you know your Grandpa Gene was a problem drinker, Karla? They say it has some hereditary factors. Some of our ancestors have been known to overindulge."

Karla looked at him as if to acknowledge that was a good one.

"I'm proud you found some help, Karla, and made such an important decision on your own for your well-being," Margaret said.

Zach stood a few steps back and stayed out of the conversation. Karla caught his eye and winked. They all started laughing.

"I could use a shower. Do you guys mind if I go to my room and get cleaned up?"

"I'm so glad you're home, honey." John laughed some more.

"Me too, John. I'll see you guys in a little bit, okay?" Karla knew staying in part would be a great challenge.

******

(September 17, 2016, 5:22 p.m.)

"I can't explain it, but I know I can't stay here anymore. I guess I have to live on my terms without you guys always being there for me when I stumble or fall. I need to know I can take care of myself without my last name always bailing me out. I've decided to leave in the morning."

"Well, where are you going to go, Karla?" Her Mom asked in that same worried tone as if she was first enlisting in the Marines.

"I don't know yet, but I promise I'll reach out to you when I find it."

"Karla. That's the craziest thing I've ever heard. Let's plan together instead of just going off half-cocked, not knowing where you'll end up." John Pillsbury has never done anything uncalculated. He couldn't, he knew exactly where she would end up. Staying in part had become second nature for all of them and it will make it more believable when needed in the future.

"That's just it, Dad; I need some crazy impulsiveness. I feel like a caged lion. I can take care of myself."

"I know Karla, you have always been a strong independent woman."

"I'll be alright, John." Her role had become so familiar that not calling him dad didn't even feel right anymore.

******

(September 18, 2016, 7:33 a.m.)

Karla left by foot from John and Margaret's elaborate

underground home on the following day, certain of the destination that lay ahead of her, part of her new mission plan. Her backpack was filled with the bare essentials. She'd traveled with less. Walking into town felt surreal. The streets moved at a light early morning flow.

As she entered the front entrance of the train station, a map of the United States hung framed on the wall. Karla's eyes naturally maneuvered toward Minneapolis, remembering her actual museum trips with her real grandparents. She was the only real Pillsbury in the group. The fond memories of going into the secret places marked employees only that now have become part of this larger plan.

"A one-way ticket to Minneapolis, Minnesota, please." Karla placed her debit card into the chip reader, and a paper ticket slid out of the slot to her waiting fingers.

******

Present day, 468
Norad Mountain Sanctuary

Karla placed her right hand down inside her pants pocket, touching the eleven-year medallion. She recalled her last meeting at the A-lano Club in Minneapolis. It became clear as a bell, remembering the faces that sat with her around the rectangular tables. Then they switched in shape and form to the ones she saw the day she and Reese had stopped there.

"This is an undetectable geo-tracking diode. My surgeon will install it under the bicep muscle of your right arm. We've re-established a useable link with one of the old decommissioned SpaceX communication satellites. After you're captured, I will be able to track your location at all times. Are you sure you want to follow through with this Karla? I'll never forgive myself if something happens to you." Elan was troubled by the decision.

"I live for this kind of action."

Elan just shook his head. "Injecting you with the bio-agent

will turn you into a super spreader. It will be undetectable and quickly contaminate every Asian individual the virus contacts. All you have to do is figure out how to get close enough to the enemies' leadership on the front line."

"Once I allow them to capture me, I'm pretty sure I will be escorted to stand in front of their top officers for questioning. If we're lucky, maybe one of them will travel back to China before detecting the virus. Or they might even take me there."

"Jesus, Karla, do you realize what we're doing?" Elan suddenly came to grips with the potential devastation of their actions.

"War is hell, Elan. Besides, they started it."

******

Day 470
The Front, Inside Chinese Held Territory

Karla spent the remainder of the afternoon preparing herself. She had taken some extra theater classes for fun while in Minneapolis, Minnesota, in between her other duties. Dressing up as a wounded soldier would require more commitment. Cuts and bruises in all the right places gave onlookers the impression she was injured in the field and had triaged her own wounds. She acted as though she was lost and disorientated from a head injury.

"Zhi, Tingzhi!" Four Chinese soldiers surrounded the wounded Marine, and Karla raised one hand in the air while holding the other arm to her side. She had purposefully dislocated it which was excruciatingly painful and placed it into a homemade sling.

One of the soldiers pushed her from behind, making her stumble forward to the ground. Then she was picked up again and forcibly escorted down a road lined with the scattered remains of burnt cars and trucks. Karla laughed inside, knowing every one of her new captors would become deathly ill in just a few short days. The plan was working perfectly, until they stopped again and one of the men got right up into Karla's face and stared. His right hand moved up her arm and then covered her breast. He smiled at her as he felt her breath wisp across his face as she slowly exhaled.

******

Karla woke up in a small dark room. She could see the outline of a food tray with three different shapes: a bowl, a plate, and a spoon. The light shined through a rectangular slot built into the bottom of the steel door.

The four soldiers had raped her. Every part of her body ached. The emotional toll was too much for Karla to suppress. Tears flowed in silence. She wouldn't give her captors the satisfaction of knowing they hurt her. The sounds of a chair moving away from a table and then footsteps outside the door caused Karla to freeze and quickly wipe her eyes and face with her shirt sleeve. Jingling keys and metal hitting against metal opened the door, making her squint in the brighter light.

An unusually large-sized female Chinese soldier stood in the doorway. She spoke poor English, ordered Karla to get up, and motioned for her to step out of the room.

A crude showerhead hung down from the ceiling. "Dress, dress," the guard motioned for her to remove her clothing.

The biological agent was already at work inside the woman, seeking out and destroying healthy cell tissue. Karla understood the woman and started to undress. The soldier noticed Karla struggling to remove her shirt, having a dislocated shoulder. She gently pulled the shirt sleeve off and helped her with the rest of her clothes. She gasped after seeing Karla's bruised chest and legs and then spoke out angrily in her native language. It became evident to Karla that the woman disapproved of her fellow soldiers' criminal treatment, but it was too late for compassion. Within days she would be deathly sick and pass unaware of what happened.

Cleaned and dressed in a one-piece gray jumpsuit, the woman escorted Karla down several hallways to a medical facility where a male doctor and a female nurse provided her with proper medical attention. They laid her out on a flat observation table and reset her shoulder. Karla bore through the pain, and the nurse handed her a small paper cup filled with a multi-color cache of pills. Karla hesitated, not knowing what she was consuming, but the young nurse smiled and nodded as if to say, it's alright; it's just vitamins. Then she reached forward and patted Karla's stomach, and with arms crossed like she was rocking a baby, she shook her head no, smiled again, and encouraged her to take the pills and drink the water.

Karla's intuition caused her to think maybe one of the pills was to prevent unnecessary pregnancies. She downed the cup and drank most of the plastic bottle of water.

The male doctor installed zip-strip handcuffs around her wrists and then left the room, and the nurse spent the rest of their time together combing Karla's tangled hair with a brush and cleaned her fingernails. Karla sensed she would soon be standing in front of key military leadership.

The woman escorted her from the medical area to another hallway and through a double doorway. As the door opened, Karla looked up, noticing the room was nearly full of soldiers. The top brass sat behind a long table at the end of the room. Karla, was placed in a chair facing the table, she coughed twice, unable to cover her mouth because of the restraints. She could hardly contain herself. Her excitement of knowing the plan was working perfectly; soon, she would be safe back with her friends and family.

An interpreter asked Karla to state her full name into a microphone set by her side.

"First Sergeant, Karla Pillsbury, United States Marine 3912548654."

"We hope you will cooperate with us today, Miss Pillsbury. We realize your President and your military are in a state of weakness and that we hold a tactical advantage that will soon cause your surrender. There is no need for any further bloodshed. We were hoping you could deliver our terms to your President. Will you do this for us, Karla Pillsbury?"

Karla realized that she would be set free to accomplish this. "What do you want me to tell them?" She asked.

"Here is a list of our demands for surrender. Take this envelope to your President Baylor."

"Okay, I'll do it." Karla noticed one of the officers sitting at the table got up and nodded to the official sitting in the center of the table. She looked around the room to see if she could identify any of the four men who assaulted her. She recognized the first man. He already looked sickly. Slightly paled face and unable to hold direct eye contact.

She spoke up again. "Can you take me closer to the front line? I'll find my way to the President as soon as possible once I make contact with my fellow soldiers."

The sound of a helicopter lifted off just outside the building, the sound faded. It flew west toward the ocean. Karla wondered if this lone messenger would be responsible for spreading the contagion to the entire Chinese Naval Fleet and then onto their homeland. Karla's involvement in this diabolical plan caused her to question why she had been chosen to fulfill this mission. God's will?

******

Day 472
Norad Mountain Sanctuary

Karla saluted her Commander and Chief and handed the sealed envelope directly into his hands. "These are terms for our surrender, Sir. I'm guessing they're now trying to figure out why so many of their people are getting sick."

"I think we can discard these into the oval file. Thank you for your heroic valor, Karla; you've saved the country. Are you okay? Is there anything you need?"

"I'd like to go on leave and actually spend some time with Reese if that's okay, Sir?"

"Karla! You are officially on leave until you decide to come back. If you don't, I'll grant you an honorable discharge, and you can go start your life over again."

"Thank you, Sir! I appreciate that very much."

PLAUSIBLE DENIABILITY

Day 468

Mindoro, Wisconsin

"We couldn't find him, Sue. We lost his trail before we got to West Salem. Did Jake ever tell either of you where that cabin was that he stayed at after the accident?" Mike was showing signs of anxiety and worry for his old friend.

"No, I guess he never did say!" Sue replied. Ailyn shook her head no.

"Maybe he'll come back. Let's wait a few days. Hopefully, he'll come to his senses." Ace suggested.

******

Ace keyed the handheld microphone of the Ham radio. "No, he just took off on us a few days ago and hasn't come back. We think he went to a cabin near where we lost a couple of friends in a vehicle accident, but he never told us where that was."

President Baylor replied. "Well, maybe he just needs some time, Ace."

"Any news you can share with me about the invasion?"

"Well." President Baylor, suddenly realized the information might be too sensitive and paused before answering the question. "We have a strategic plan in place today that will change the outcome of the invasion back in our favor. I should have some more information to share with you in the coming days."

"Oh, okay." Ace sensed the president was withholding valuable information from him. He thought that even as Governor, he wouldn't always be allowed total disclosure. "Are we pushing the opposition forces off American soil, or should we be prepared to fight them in Wisconsin?"

President Baylor laughed out loud. "Trust me, Ace. They will wish they would have stayed in their homeland when we're through with them."

******

Day 475
Mindoro, WI.

The pilot brought the Chinook down onto the Sanderson landing pad.

Karla's anticipation to see Reese was real to her, she exited the rear cargo door and ran into Reese's waiting arms. She looked around for Patch. "Where's Patch? I've missed him so much, but not as much as I've missed you, Reese!" Karla hugged him and gave him another kiss before he was able to answer the question.

"Patch is with Alphonsa Orlov, Karla. He's, his dog."

Karla took a second for that new information to register. "Really?"

"Yeah, after we left the museum, we stopped there, and Patch ran right into Mr. Orlov's arms. It turns out he is the descendant of a famous Russian dog that went up into space. Reese refrained from telling her about the lost chess game.

"So, he was his dog?"

"Yes."

"Well, that sucks." Karla showed apparent signs of disappointment and sadness. "It's not like dogs are just everywhere anymore. You can't just go down to the fuckin pound and adopt another one." She started to cry. Reese held her tight, happy to have her in his arms and to feel useful again.

Dan and Ailyn had given their son time to greet Karla alone. They walked up to the landing pad and saw the raw emotions.

"Are you guys, okay? What's wrong, Karla?" Ailyn asked, concerned.

Karla stepped away from Reese and went to hug Ailyn and Dan.

"I just learned about Patch and wasn't quite ready to hear that. It's so good to see you guys!" Karla hugged them both.

Dan could see and sensed something different in Karla. Maybe he would never honestly know what she experienced, but whatever it was, it physically took a toll on her. He never publicly talked about a woman's age, but it appeared that Karla lost ten years in her face and hands from her recent experiences.

The pilot wheeled a wooden shipping container down the cargo ramp onto a cement pad and waved to Dan as he walked back out of sight. The engine started, and the long blades began to turn, lifting the helicopter back off the ground. It leaned slightly forward and began to carry itself horizontally away from the hillside.

"Come on, let's go catch up inside," Ailyn said as the noise started to fade.

"The fighting has stopped. Will you be able to stay with me?" Reese asked the preemptive question about their future.

"Yeah, Reese, I'm done. Let's get married and settle down someplace and start over."

Reese stopped her on the path to the bunker door and turned toward Karla. He grabbed both her hands, knelt in front of her, and proposed. "Karla, will you marry me?"

"Didn't we do this once already?" Karla smiled down at him. "Yes!"

Ailyn and Dan both started to cry. The raw emotions were just too much for them to conceal. All four ended up in a group hug that switched back to laughter.

Day 473
Norad Mountain Sanctuary

From a short distance, the Mexican naval vessels witnessed firsthand several Chinese ships adrift as none appeared in control.

A large destroyer had run aground off the shores of Tijuana and was listing portside - all its engines were still running.

Radio communications slowly made their way to President Baylor's ears. He had decided plausible deniability would be the best course of action. At the present moment, only he, Elan Must, and Karla Pillsbury knew what transpired to cause such human destruction.

Unfortunately, American citizens affected by the virus also fell victim—unavoidable casualties from an untested delivery system. Thousands became deathly ill and passed.

A decision, second-guessed, and the short timing, made it impossible to supply his fellow Asian-American citizens with the antidote serum. The untimely news devastated President

Baylor's mind, leaving him with restless nights and little sleep. He wasn't sure he would ever forgive himself. Only one person was responsible. Baylor put it all on Regina Putman.

THE PUTMANS

Day 480, 7:00 p.m.

*Little St. James Island,
U.S. Virgin Islands*

"Alex, I've got a little surprise planned for your birthday."

"Really? Regina, I love surprises."

Just then, a flash grenade came crashing through the picture window and exploded with a loud bang. The Putmans both covered their ears and fell to the floor. Their outside security personnel had already been incapacitated and were unable to offer any further assistance as Seal Team Nine's sniper members had strategically eliminated them as threats.

Two other members of the Putman security team, posted inside the dwelling had let their guard down. They had succumbed to similar fates; unaware due to the laxed duty they had experienced since arriving onto the island paradise.

Four Navy Seals entered the unlocked Dutch doors, guns raised into firing positions. They proceeded to force each man down to the ground, placing their arms behind their backs and attaching zip ties around their wrists.

The same scenario took place in the open living area of the residence, where both Putmans unwillingly found themselves constrained and physically removed from their residence to the tiled patio by the pool.

Regina Putman, demanded an explanation. "Do you know who we are? Why are you doing this? Under who's authority?"

The senior officer in charge interrupted her. "Regina and Alex Putman, you are both under arrest and are being charged with espionage and treason for conspiring with foreign governments against The United States of America.

"You have no proof of this. I don't know what you're talking about." Regina was visibly upset and it displayed through her vocal tone.

"What have you done, Regina?" Alex went down to his knees, the look of anguish on his face, he knew the jig was up.

"Shut up Alex, they don't know a thing, keep your mouth shut, you hear me?"

Looking directly at the soldier who stood over his shoulder. "It was all her. Regina planned it all. She planned all of this with terrorists from the Middle East. I didn't have anything to do with it." Alex Putman pleaded with the soldier.

"Damn it, Alex, I told you to shut the hell up." Catching her constrainer off guard, Regina moved quickly in her husbands direction. She kicked her right foot forward striking the point of her shoe squarely against his left temple. Alex Putman fell sideways into the deep section of the pool.

Everyone stood for a brief second, pausing from the unexpected event. Alex's body sank through the disturbed water to the bottom of the pool. He was unconscious. The water color slowly turned a pinkish hew clouding clear visibility from above.

The soldier closest to the edge placed his weapons down and jumped into the water toward the sunken body. The poolside onlookers could see him struggling to drag the former President toward the shallow depths of the inground pool. He lifted the body up and held it against the tiled walls where two other soldiers lifted it onto the surrounding walkways. A visible blood line began to flow freely down the left cheekbone of his face. Regina's pointed dress shoe had penetrated her husbands temple and it appeared as though his neck might have been broken.

First aid measures were immediately administered, but the damage was too extensive. Former President Alex Putman was dead.

"He's dead, you've killed your husband, Mrs. Putman," said one of the soldiers who attempted to provide lifesaving measures.

Regina's face contorted. She was caught in between frustration and empathy. Then it came, a wailing sound none of the men had ever experienced before. A sound only a demon possessed human could make. The look on her face changed back to obstinance and aggression. A look of pure disgust.

"Now you are also charged with murder, Mrs. Putman."

It took four physically fit soldiers to restrain the thrashing prisoner. A sedative was finally administered to help constrain her. They bound her legs and carried her to the piers and placed her onto the floor of their Mark V SOC, (Special Operations Craft).

****

"I don't understand Regina? Millions of people died because of what you did. Was it worth it? Tomorrow you're going to be hung, but for what? Money, power, greed? May God have mercy on your soul." President Baylor turned and began to walk away from the steel door. He could hear her breathing.

"Fuck you, Baylor! I hope you rot in hell." The gravelly

voice leaked from inside the cell.

President Baylor stopped, turned around and looked her in the eyes from outside the small rectangular window. "No, Regina, you're the only one here with a spot reserved in hell."

Regina lunged toward the light; her face pressed tightly against the open window slot. Foam lathered from the sides of her lips.

Baylor fell slightly backwards, then regained his composure. He turned and slowly walked away from the cell as Regina Putman, or what seemed to be left of her, babbled out in a foreign language, unrecognizable to the living.

****

Day 500, 12:00p.m.
Norad Sanctuary

President Baylor stood on top of the wooden gallows, constructed the day after Seal Team Nine arrested her on Little St. James Island.

Regina, shuffled forward in leg irons and a black head covering. She was escorted by two guards. They removed the leg irons but kept her hands bound. A sturdy hemp rope noose was slipped down over her head around her neck and the knot was adjusted. The black head covering was then removed and she squinted to focus her eyes from the blinding noonday sunlight.

"Regina Putman, you have been found guilty of a multitude of heinous crimes against humanity, and treasonous acts against the United States of America. As punishment for these criminal acts, you will now be hung by the neck until dead. Do you have any last words?" President Baylor looked straight into her eyes, seeing what might be remorse on the woman's tired face. He asked once more in a softer voice. "Do you have anything you wish to say, Regina? Any last words before you meet your Maker?"

"Yes, yes I do, Mitch." She seemed to have come to a new level of acceptance in her voice and facial expressions. "You all can go to hell!"

President Baylor nodded to the executioner with his readied hands on the wooden handle. A trap door flung down away from Regina's waiting feet. She dropped quickly as gravity pulled her body weight down the open square hole toward the sandy soil below. A loud crack could be heard from most of the onlookers in the crowd nearest to the wooden platform. Her body writhed and shook, swinging from side to side like the counter weights on a grandfather clock. The movement lessened and finally stopped, meeting her final fate. Reaping what's sown, suffering the consequences of her own behavior.

The crowd initially gasped, turned, and then looked on again in horror. No one in this crowd had ever experienced anything like this before as the last public hanging performed as a method of capital punishment occurred in 1936. A new law had passed in January of 2025 allowing this type of punishment again in America if the country was actively under martial law and acts of treason were involved.

Regina Putmans body was buried next to her husbands in an unmarked grave outside of the Norad Mountain sanctuary.

President Baylor felt no remorse at that moment.

WISH I COULD HAVE BEEN THERE

Day 500, 3:30 p.m.

Melrose, Wisconsin

"Are you okay, President Baylor?" Ace asked out of caring.

"Yes, so much death and destruction, Ace. I thought ordering Regina Putman's execution would provide me with some closure, but I'm experiencing the exact opposite. She was almost solely responsible for the attacks on our country and yet, now, I'm remorseful having exercised her public hanging. Maybe I wanted her to suffer more than that. Is that wrong, Ace?"

"Oh, I don't know. She certainly reaped what she sowed and it's my guess the fire and brimstone experience for all of eternity in hell might be more punishment than anything you could have done to her physically or mentally in revenge for her actions. I wish I could have been there. You know I saw her and former President Putman in an unusual paranormal experience that I had on the day the bomb forced us underground."

"Oh, yeah. How did you do that?" President Baylor sounded shocked and inquisitive to hear what his newest Governor was about to say next, and Ace began to share the story details complete. "So, this out of body experience put you right in front of them by their pool, and she acted as though she saw you?"

"I know it sounds crazy, but it is exactly as I described." Ace felt awkward and unsure of the President's belief.

"Pretty strange, Ace. Far be it from me to doubt you. I bet your wife and the Sandersons freaked out a little."

"We all let it go and I've never brought the topic up in

conversation again until right now. Like I said before, I can't explain why these things happen to me, but they always seem to be for the greater good."

"Well, like I said before, I'm just glad I've got you on my side, Ace." President Baylor snickered and it came through clearly over the Ham radio speaker.

The two men signed off and Ace joined the others inside the new garden area. He was amazed in such a short time period of time how fast the vegetables had grown already. They would possibly be eating off some of the plants in less than a month. The rabbits and their cages were moved into a separated adjoining room connected to the domed shelter. There were plans to include a male and a female goat, some chickens and two pigs. Feed would be brought in by helicopter and stored inside what remained of the steel pole barn, which had some new repairs done by a work crew and Mike's supervision.

"Well, I just learned from President Baylor that Regina and Alex Putman are both dead. The world won't have to be concerned about future attacks from the likes of them again. China has been neutralized and also is no longer going to be a threat. I think it's peacetime and we can truly work on re-building again." Ailyn walked over and hugged her husband and smiled up at him. Everyone seemed to take a sigh of relief.

Mike mentioned, Jake. "I hope he's alright, where ever he ended up."

"Yeah, who knows? Everybody keep him in your thoughts and prayers, okay?" Ace had an unusual feeling sweep over him as he walked back outside. He couldn't feel if their old friend was still alive. Not like the feeling he had about Hatty and Reese. Time will tell.

WEDDINGS AND VIDEO GAMES

Day 509, 8:30 a.m.

Dallas, Texas

John Pillsbury and his family were busy decorating and preparing for the planned wedding of their only daughter. Invitations were sent out by radio and helicopter delivery. Margaret Pillsbury was as busy as a one-armed paper hanger and come hell or high water she was going to make this wedding the biggest thing next to sliced bread. Afterall, it's only going to happen once that she gets to see Karla in a long train white wedding gown.

"They should be here around five o'clock today, honey," Margaret said excitedly to her husband.

"I'm looking forward to meeting the Ayers. They have been through a lot together. I hope we can all breathe a little easier now that the threat is over. Maybe we can get things back to normal again." John Pillsbury smiled and grabbed the plastic tote of wedding decorations from off the table.

"Zach, give me a hand hanging these around the room, please." The paper wedding bells opened and hooked together. They were of varying sizes and shapes with a silvery gleam. "It looks like we have twice as many of the bigger sized bells compared to these smaller ones. How about if we put two like this and hang the smaller one between them."

"I really don't care. They look fine to me." Zach was playing the part of a single young man, still living with his parents because of the circumstances the world has been forced to endure. He was happy for Karla, but didn't really want to be saddled with the responsibility of helping to do any of the decorating. Zach had made new friends in the community.

John's ability to recognize the sudden lack of interest and the realization of just how unfair life seemed for Zach to be stuck in his role these last two years gave him a feeling of empathy. "I tell you what, Zach, if you help me finish hanging these bells, mainly holding the ladder steady for me, then you can go hang out with your friends for the rest of the day if you want."

Zach looked at the six totes of decorations and thought about his selfish motives. He reconsidered John's offer. "I'm sorry Dad, no I'll stay and help out until you and mom are done."

Margaret hearing the conversation, walked over to her two men and expressed her gratitude to them both for actively chipping in on the task. The three of them worked efficiently together until the job was done. The recreation hall looked like the feature pages from inside the magazine 'Tomorrow's Bride.' They stood together before hitting the elevator door button and admired their labor of love.

"Great job, guys. Doesn't it look fantastic, thank you for helping me. I couldn't have done it without you."

"We've got your back, Mom." Zach smiled at John.

****

The chinook helicopters arrived at few minutes before five o'clock. Dan and Ailyn Ayer stepped off the cargo ramp first, followed by Hatty and her husband Darin and their girls. Reese and Karla followed behind them and quickly moved past the group to greet the Pillsbury family on the brick pathway that led off the landing pad.

"Hi Mom. Hi Dad." Karla gave them both a prolonged hug. She took charge of all the introductions and everyone slowly brushed off the uncomfortableness of first impressions.

Margaret Pillsbury was as ready for company as she could be and encouraged everyone to follow her inside their home.

Dan and Ailyn couldn't help but notice how different the parents of the bride's property looked and felt in comparison to their own. The green grass, manicured with not a single blade of grass out of place. The perfectly aligned fence posts that stretched out further than their eyes could see into the horizon line. Texas was lucky to not endure any backlash from the fires and winds. It all became too much for Ailyn to handle emotionally, she stopped and tears began to fall from her eyes. Margaret took notice of the sudden change in emotions and reached out to hold her new friend and console her.

"I don't know exactly why you're crying, Ailyn, but that's okay. When you're ready, let's have a little chat about it, I'm here for you, my friend."

Ailyn, wiped her eyes with the back of her hand, accidentally smudging her make-up. She was going to need some extra attention with Margaret's help before proceeding with the family to their living quarters.

"John, take everyone downstairs for me, please. I'm going to stop on our floor to spend some quality time with Ailyn." The elevator was large enough to accommodate everyone at once as it served to deliver even the largest pieces of machinery and materials to the six levels inside.

The back wall of the elevator opened onto the third floor and Margaret, arms still around Ailyn's shoulders, stepped off. "We'll see yawl in a little while."

John Pillsbury did his best to proceed forward with his original plans to comfortably transition his guests into their rooms for the short weekend stay. "Three more floors down, everyone."

The elevator door opened and the newcomers had similar expressions on their faces that Reese had his first time, only this time the main recreation hall was decorated for a wedding.

"This is amazing, John. When did you build your bunker?" Dan asked.

"Margaret and I broke ground in 1998. It's been a labor of love ever since. I'll give you a full tour later, if you're interested."

"I'd like that very much."

"Okay, Darin and Hatty and the girls are there at the last

door on the right. Dan, you and Ailyn will have your own room on the other side. You'll be sharing the floor with President Baylor and Maggie, and Elan Must in the other two rooms. I hope you don't mind?"

"Oh, heck no, it will give us a chance to get to know each other better. I couldn't think of a better way to spend New Year's Eve." Dan was especially excited to have this opportunity. It might be the first time everyone would be able to relax and truly be themselves.

"If you don't mind, I have some things to attend to upstairs, then I will bring Margaret and Ailyn back down with me in a little while. There's a fully stocked kitchen right there, so please help yourself to anything you can find. Girls, how long has it been since you've played any video games?"

Annie and Emma looked at each other with a look of surprise. Emma, asked Mr. Pillsbury, "Do you have Mario Cart?"

"That's one of Zach and my favorites, Emma. There's a game station in your room. When I get time, we'll have a race." The girls both headed toward the open doorway and disappeared.

"Well, we won't see them for a while." Darin said and laughed.

"I'll be back in a little while. Please make yourselves at home." The elevator doors closed and the red numbers began their count backwards from six to one.

****

Saturday, January 1, 2028
Dallas, Texas

Reese stood at the front of the seated guests, more on the bride's side of the aisle then on his own.

An outside winter wedding in Texas allowed for suits and ties to be worn by most of the men, and formal wedding dresses for the women. Any other time of the year, the heat would make this type of attire extremely uncomfortable.

John Pillsbury, the handsome father of the bride impatiently waited outside the front entrance of his riding arena, where Margaret, Ailyn and Hatty and her step daughters were attending to Karla's last second preparations. They turned their attention to the soft knocking sounds on the metal door as it opened and the rooms lighting changed to a mixture of LED fluorescents and natural sunshine.

"It's time girls, everyone's here and waiting for us."

Annie and Emma grabbed ahold of Hatty and started making their way out alongside the chairs and quickly took their seats on the groom's side.

Dan held out his arm to Ailyn and he escorted her down to their seats in the front row. It only took one look into their son's eyes and both of them succumbed to joyful tears.

Rascal Flat's 'Bless The Broken Road' started to play from the speakers as Karla, escorted by her parents, came around the corner of the steel sided building into full view of the now standing guests.

Reese tried to stand still, but couldn't as he felt like a strong breeze gently pushed against his face and chest. It was the first time in a day he had seen his bride-to-be. Her beauty overtook him with emotions and anticipation, readjusting his stance to a sense of stability then catching each other's gaze, they smiled.

Karla's long white train of her wedding dress lay out behind her, flowing like waves on the ocean. It swept fragrant bluebell pedals randomly in her path, dropped by a young flower girl.

John Pillsbury kissed his only daughter and honorably handed her over to the care of a man he hardly knew, but in his heart, he had no doubt, would care for Karla from now on.

The Minister, Reverend Paul Long, is the pastor of a small community church in the nearby town that the Pillsbury's had become an intricate part of since moving to Texas. "Dear family and friends, welcome on behalf of the Pillsbury and Ayer families on this blessed day of celebration to unite Reese and Karla in holy matrimony."

The ceremony continued with barely a dry eye left seated, evident that these special experiences in New America had been devoid of such traditional celebration.

"You may kiss the bride!"

Everyone cheered and clapped as they stood to their feet congratulating the newly married couple.

Reese and Karla walked together back up the aisle, followed by both sets of parents. They formed a receiving line near the end of the red brick walkway that led to the bunker entrance and elevator doors.

Reverend Long announced directions to the waiting guests and each row dismissed singularly through the receiving line. The elevator held a total of twenty-four persons at a time, which delivered them comfortably down the six floors to the reception hall.

****

The door's opened and once again the cheers could have been heard at ground level, as Reese and Karla stepped forward into their reception hall. They didn't even get to sit down at the head table before sounds of silverware clinking on crystal glasses caused them both to enter into a warm embrace and kiss. Reese bent his new bride down in a dip and lifted her back up which made everyone cheer once more.

Ace looked over at Ailyn and snuck a quick kiss himself. "Did you ever think he would get married, honey?"

"Oh yeah, he just needed to meet the right one." Ailyn smiled.

RUSSIA'S PEACEKEEPER

Day 510, January 1, 2028

Red Wing, Minnesota

"Have you considered with what's happened up until this moment, how compromised the world powers truly are. We won't ever gain another opportunity like this again, Alphonsa. Mother Russia is in the strongest position militarily that it's ever been. We are for once the strongest superpower. A calculated attack now against the United States would allow us world domination," boasted President Palarov, who showed signs of inebriation from his Russian vodka highball.

Alphonsa Orlov, paused for a moment before answering. Hearing this alarming statement from the one man who he had once thought to be Russia's peacekeeper. He reset his position in his highbacked leather office chair and spoke freely. "President Palarov, you of all people surprise me to hear such thinking out loud. I could ask you plainly, why now, why ever? Your entire platform has been achieved from a position of compromise and bi-partisan effort. The people were ready for a change and you delivered it. These people who have survived with me in this bunker all came to America disillusioned by the corruption of the governments of the past. I can speak for all of them. They don't want any more fighting. Enough was enough with the Ukraine/ United States war. Why can't we become part of the rebuilding process. Succumbing to the dirty tactics of the past that all stem from power and greed is what's gotten the world into this position."

President Palarov's countenance changed and he lowered his eyes toward the ground. "Forgive me Alphonsa. I've always respected your opinion and never want anything to disrupt our friendship. Our families have been fighting arm and arm for generations. I'm not sure what came over me. Former President Pruett and I had a solid working relationship. Helping Baylor secure America's borders came with less of a cost to our fighting soldiers than I expected. Acquiring Alaska is a game changer for Russia. Just the mineral rights alone will place us in a dynamic position after the world has fully recovered."

"As long as he and Must and their new formulation of government doesn't screw it all up again, we should be in a humanitarian position unlike anything the world has ever experienced. After the takeover of coastal lands in Ukraine distributing markets for oil and gas have doubled, everything changed for the betterment of the human race." Alphonsa, paused and sipped from his white tea cup, while Palarov finished the last swallow out of the tall glass tumbler.

"Who released the deadly viral pathogen that was used to wipe out the Chinese forces of aggression? Do you think that was, Baylor?"

"I don't know yet, but it certainly would be a fair question to ask the next time one of us meets with him privately. I had heard Mrung had secret bio-engineering experiments performed while he was in office. How ever it happened, we should never underestimate what human beings are capable of when facing imminent danger."

"So, we are in agreement then? Let's work with Baylor and the world leaders instead of fighting to take it all over for a change."

Palarov nodded, "yes, good my friend." Alphonsa felt his breathing and countenance change.

****

President Palarov flew Northwest. His Mil MI-10 helicopter, a technological marvel re-designed and improved off the MI-8 platform. It quietly gained altitude and disappeared over the Minnesota bluffs that ran along the Mississippi River valley. His destination coordinates set for Juneau, Alaska where he planned on meeting with several of the state's legislative members and Governor Caylan to discuss terms for ownership transfer. Knowing none of them were going to be too happy to see him nor will they be willing or likely to fully cooperate without concessions. He was now fully prepared to do what was right for all parties concerned.

****

Governor Caylan stood up from behind the radio desk, "Sir, I'm not sure you understand the gravity of the situation. None of us are happy with what you've done. I realize you made an executive decision based on the circumstances you found yourself and the country to be in at that moment, but without speaking with me first seems highly irregular. How can you expect us to just give up our entire state to the Russian Government?" President Baylor stayed silent, hoping the old adage was true, whoever speaks first loses. Governor Caylan started in again after the uncomfortable seconds of radio silence. "Palarov is due any minute now. You say he is willing to negotiate for peace and cooperation, and you trust him, Mr. President?"

President Baylor paused again, then decided his next course of action should be direct and succinct. "Governor Caylan, I can understand and appreciate how you must feel.

Given the circumstances, if I were in your shoes, I may feel the same way. It's obvious to me that if you chose to be combative and stifle communication with President Palarov, ultimately, he may have no other choice but to take what is now rightfully his by force, leaving you with nothing. Is that what you really think will be in the best interests of Alaska right now, Sarah? Hear him out and see what he has in mind. Maybe for once we can all just finally get along with each other?"

The Governor could tell from the tone in the president's voice, he no longer cared what happens next to Alaska. "He's here, Sir. I'll touch base with you afterwards if you don't mind? Juneau, Alaska, over and out."

****

Sarah Caylan approached the helicopter pad, hand extended, to properly greet the man who fundamentally changed Russia. The wind caused by the slowing blades lifted the hairs not caught fully into her hair clip and she felt the need to brush them back down the sides of her head as she put on a happy face for her new guest. "Welcome to Juneau, Alaska, President Palarov. Please follow me. I've prepared a comfortable place for us to meet and talk."

"Thank you, Governor, Caylan. It is a pleasure to finally meet you in person. I have been an admirer of your political career. Not many politicians become elected to the governor's position for multiple terms during their time in office. The citizens of Alaska must appreciate what you do for them very much?"

"I appreciate you saying that, Mr. President. How long has it been since you have eaten. Can I treat you to a special dinner reception either before or after our meeting?"

"Afterwards will be exceptional, thank you, I accept your invitation."

The entourage filed into a medium sized conference room. Many of the state legislators were already inside awaiting the arrival of their guest. Eager, but apprehensive to take part in a negotiation process that affects their lives and livelihood. Everyone stood out of respect and waited for the Russian President to take his seat at the head of the table. Governor Caylan sat next to him on his right side and made her best attempt of introduction to allow him to speak freely.

"Thank you, Governor Caylan. As you have all painfully learned, your President Baylor and I were placed in an awkward but necessary position, forced to make a very difficult decision. Your President was trapped in a corner by the Chinese attack on your country. When we met to discuss an alliance, I was committing brave men and women soldiers from Russia to fight and potentially give their lives to prevent China from world domination. I realize our two countries have long been at odds against each other and not always living in peaceable terms, but I can assure you now as a man of integrity, your lives will not be negatively affected by what's happened. I promise you will be able to proceed with your daily functions just as before. Stay in your homes, work, hunt, fish, and play, interact with us as fellow human beings working to accomplish a new goal for peace and goodwill to all. President Baylor and I, the Governors of your country and the leaders of the rest of the surviving mother earth are going to unite, once and for all, to live in peace together and work for the common good of all parties concerned. No more poverty, no more hunger, no more fighting. Alaska is rich with resources and they will be used for the betterment of the world at large. No more decisions based on money, power and greed. So, I ask you all, can you do this with me?"

Most inside the room could be seen sharing various positive gestures in response to what they just heard. How will it be possible? Is it possible? One world, one people, all living in harmony together for the greater good of each other's needs. Unselfish desires for peace.

Governor Caylan stood and thanked everyone for coming and then made the first attempt at moving forward thru optimism. She could see a select few of her state's leadership weren't showing the same enthusiasm in giving up control. She would try to fix this over time. "President Palarov, let's go enjoy a nice meal together and finalize some more of the planned details."

****

Less people occupied the world's continents because of a select few region's quest for power and control. The people who lived in the Middle East, China, Eastern Australia, and most of Eastern Asia had been wiped out either by aggression or tidal wave. The landscape of the western United States had geographically been altered by the devastating earthquakes caused by the nuclear detonations. Leaders from the countries that remained planned to meet and discuss the future. Only a few American and Russian satellites were saved and re-routed into a safe trajectory rotation around the earth, away from the debris fields. Vital communication links were re-established that allowed world leaders to coordinate their efforts more efficiently. At the moment it seemed like the future was looking brighter for those who've survived. A summit date and location was set.

G-10 SUMMIT

Day 546, February 5, 2028

Panama City, Panama

"Have you ever seen such a beautiful view, Maggie?" President Baylor let go of his new bride's hand and walked to the panoramic view from the top floor of their Bristol Hotel suite.

"It's breathtaking," Maggie answered back.

"Almost as if none of what's happened even exists. I mean looking at this makes it seem like what we experienced was just a bad dream." Pausing for a moment of reflection. "I'm going to step down as president, Maggie."

"What?"

"Yeah, I've made my decision. I'll break the news to Elan after the summit is finalized."

"Will he take over your position?"

"That's up to him. Either Elan or John Pillsbury or maybe Dan Ayer." Maggie shook her head from side to side. "What? You don't like the idea?"

Maggie smiled, "I'll go where ever you go Mr. President!"

****

Day 547, February 6, 2028
Bristol Hotel Convention Center
Panama City, Panama

President Mitch Baylor looked down to his wrist, the time read 6:59 p.m. He stopped the vibrating alarm on his watch and stood to excuse himself from his dinner table seat to approach the podium at the front of the large meeting room. Almost all the leaders from every surviving country were in attendance. The G-10 Summit was about to get started. Some noticed him adjusting the microphone and stopped their conversations. Baylor felt that uncomfortable rise in perspiration levels common for him when addressing crowds or when under stress.

"Ladies and Gentleman, if I may have your attention, please. Let's get started if we may?" Those individuals unable to understand the English language looked down onto the tables in front of them where an AI Translator screen automatically transcribed every word spoken in their native language along with special earpieces that spoke the words softly in their native dialect. When the crowd noise silenced, Baylor continued. "I wish to thank all of you for willingly and freely choosing to meet together. We are aiming toward the fulfillment of a common world goal. There's been enough violence. It's time for peace and over time, working together, with a shared vision, we can create nirvana. No more poverty, no more suffering." Heads bobbed up and down in agreement, then the crowd relaxed again.

"Everyone has their place and purpose and from now on

we all will thrive together without greed, or power, or the need of financial gain. Chosen leadership works for the benefit of the many, not the one. It's time for the inhabitants of earth to become federated." President Baylor paused and one person started clapping and it became contagious.

"I personally have no further desires to lead America into this world vision. After today, the country I love will gain new leadership at the table. Two Ambassadors that will have hearts to serve, with humility, helping us all to transition comfortably into our newly founded relationships." The crowd shuffled and stirred, surprised to hear this unexpected news.

"All of you came to the Summit fully aware and in agreement of this planned future thanks to former President Mrung. I spent many nights lying awake contemplating what my role would be. I came to the realization for the best interest of the federation, I need to step down, and pass the torch. May I be so bold to offer myself as an example to those of you who might benefit from a similar decision. Fresh attitudes, fresh outlooks. I desire for all of you to be aware of my intentions, I'll be asking our current slate of Governors to consider my Vice-President, Elan Must with either Governor John Pillsbury or Governor Dan Ayer to take their seat at the table, equally. These three men have my highest trust and confidence to represent America honorably." Once again, the crowd stirred, if the spoken words were written they would be illegible.

"Thank you, to all of you who participated today, let's raise our glasses together. To the worlds federation, Federation Earth!" The sounds of chairs being pushed back from the tables and then clinking glasses took over.

President Baylor walked down into the table area and shook hands with many in the crowd. He could hear and feel the excitement in the room. *'At last,'* He thought to himself. Thinking about the adversity it took for the world to get to this point. As if it was all meant to be. A divine plan and purpose.

****

Day 550, February 10th, 2028
Norad Mountain, Idaho

"I know I sprung this on you without warning, Ace, but the timing was right and I had a gut feeling you wouldn't say no." President Baylor sensed the anxiety building through the subtle changes in Ace's body language.

"Geez, Mr. President, don't get me wrong, I am honored you even thought this much of me much less acted upon impulse about it, but you could have sprung it on me earlier to give me a chance to think it over first. What if I said no?"

"You won't!"

Ace laughed a little, surprised at the man's over confidence. "So let me get this straight, then. John and I will co-chair a position in Federation Earth's new slate of elected leaders to represent America after you retire. Maybe Ailyn and I would like to enjoy some retirement too? Did you ever consider that?"

Baylor, didn't know if Ace's apprehension was stemming from lack of confidence and self-esteem or if he was serious. "So, you are turning me down?"

"No, I'll do it, but only if there's a term limit set up front. Say like four years, then I step down and allow for fresh blood. Maybe someone else can take my place then?"

"Great, I will make the proper arrangements and take care of all the bureaucratic formalities. Thank you Ace, for your willingness to serve your country." President Baylor smiled, making eye contact that caused Ace to think that somehow, he just got bluffed by a master poker player.

"What are you and Maggie going to do?"

"I think we are going to spend some time in the Virgin Islands. The honeymoon we never got to enjoy together, because of the chaos, and if we like it there, maybe we will stay." Now Ace, felt a little more compassion for his new friend. They both deserved to find some peace and tranquility together. This renewed his spirit and he accepted the new role completely. Ailyn might be another story?

FULL OF GOODNESS

Day 575, March 5th, 2028

Melrose, Wisconsin

"Well, this is it, Mike!" Ace stood in front of his best friend, ready to say farewell. The bunker had saved them from suffering frightening deaths.

"I can't even believe it. You are leaving all of this behind, to go off and try to save the world again." Mike laughed at his subtle attempt at humor. Obvious to both men it was meant to cover up the awkward emotions welling up from deep inside the man's heart.

"No reason why you gotta make this all weird and shit, Mike." Ace wiped a tear away from his left eye. The bond that drew the two men together will always be stronger than time separating them apart. Ace grabbed ahold of his friend and hugged him like never before. "Thank you for saving us, Mike. None of us would have made it if you didn't build the bunker."

"Yeah, it's starting to look like a little town now." Several new structures had been built with people coming and going, transitioning between safe zones and new territory. Mike and

Sue had been able to move back into their old home again, as it was completely rebuilt back to its original condition along with the pole barn.

"Are you ready to go?" Ailyn walked up the stone path to the helicopter pad where Mike and Dan stood. Obvious to her from the redness around the two men's eyes, they had just shared an intimate emotional moment together.

"Yeah, I think I'm ready, honey. Bye for now, my friends." Ace and Ailyn hugged Mike and Sue together, then turned and walked arm and arm to the ramp of their new Sikorsky S-92 executive helicopter.

Looking down, seeing their friends getting smaller, waving to them from above, the sun's reflection shone bright off the glass panels of the environmentally controlled gardens and in less than a minute Ace lost sight of the hilltop sanctuary as they neared their top cruising speed of 190 miles per hour.

****

Ace reached his hand forward to greet Alphonsa Orlov standing in front of his bunker's entranceway. This time, Alphonsa reciprocated. The two men realized the awkwardness from the varying squeeze strengths, powerful, then weak, then with acceptance, then powerful again. The chopper's blades were nearing their last revolutions as the sounds of the engines shut down.

"Hello, Alphonsa. Good to see you again. You remember, Ailyn?"

"Yes, good to see you both again. Please come inside, have you eaten dinner yet? Are you hungry?" Alphonsa politely opened the door on the right and motioned for his guests to enter.

The aroma from the kitchen wafted into Ace's nostrils, knowing it was prepared by Vladimir, the groups professional executive chef. It was impossible to turn down the invitation, as it was a rare treat to consume professionally prepared foods.

Ivan and his wife were walking together up the hallway with their newborn baby in Ivan's arms. He wore a smile from ear to ear. The proud father couldn't wait to introduce his new son to the Ayers.

Ailyn's hands moved up covering her mouth and cheeks. She had no idea there was a new baby. "Oh my God, look at this little peanut. May I?" Having an infant cradled in her arms made the world a special place again.

"Congratulations Ivan, I can tell you both are very proud. What's his name?" Ace, asked.

"Dariy!"

"That is a beautiful name, Ivan. Full of goodness, this one is." Ace reached over and stroked the boy's cheek with his finger, while Ivan and Daria looked at each other, wondering the coincidence for Ace to describe the true meaning of their son's rare name. Alphonsa caught it too, but no one elaborated on their thoughts.

Ace, placed the last fork full of Vladimir's Russian Piroshki into his mouth, a meat hand pie that sort of reminded him of the Upper Michigan pasties that he loved so much. "Vladimir, my compliments to you, Sir. That was the best meat pie I have ever eaten."

Vladimir smiled and thanked the guests for the opportunity to serve, then hurried off back into the kitchen, as if there was a fire.

"Wait until you taste dessert, Ailyn. Vladimir is an excellent baker as well. He told me he would prepare for us one of the favorite desserts served in Russian households, Napoleon Cake."

"I can't wait to try it. Dan and I try to limit our dessert consumption to stay in shape, but when we do indulge it is always such a treat."

Ivan helped Vladimir carry out the precision precut cake slices setting the plates down in front of everyone seated at the tables. When they were finished, Alphonsa stood up from his chair and raised his glass to make a toast. "Raise your glasses to celebrate our many blessings. A toast to our guests, new Federation Earth leader Daniel Ayer and first lady, Ailyn. To peace and prosperity, Boodym zdaROvy! (To our health)

****

Ace and Alphonsa retired to Alphonsa's private office while Ailyn was kept occupied paying attention to Ivan and Daria's new baby boy, Dariy. Only this time, Ace planned on asking his new friend to play a new game with a different set of rules.

"I'll get right to the point of my visit, Alphonsa." Ace sat down in the chair on the right side of the priceless hardwood desk. "Alphonsa now that I am no longer Governor of the Midwest territory, former President Baylor and I both agree that you should be offered the first opportunity at the position. Things have changed with his stepping down and retiring. What do you think about that?"

Alphonsa paused for a brief moment and looked upward, evident by his body language he was contemplating the request.

"Ace, you flatter me with your question and confidence. It is quite unexpected I have to admit. A former Russian citizen being asked to sit in such a position of importance in a newly formed world government. I truly care about our world's safety and prosperity. Humanity deserves to be free of all the fighting and struggles caused by power, greed and money. Will I have your assurance that you and Baylor will always be available to me for questions and assistance when needed?"

"Yes, twenty-four hours a day, if necessary, Alphonsa. Well, me anyway." Ace smiled.

"Well, then my answer is yes."

Ace rose from his chair and laid his right hand on Alphonsa's shoulder and then reached in to shake in agreement. It was the first game, he actually won, playing against such a worthy opponent.

TESTOSTERONE LEVELS

Day 577, March 7th, 2028

New Elmar, Wisconsin

Darin and Josh had started a new project together after Darin and his family got back from Reese and Karla's wedding in Texas.

Before the wedding, Josh mentioned to Darin that he and Penny were going to go up to Brownsville, Wisconsin, where multiple solar fields were scattered and broken from the devastation caused by the fires, wind and fallout. He felt that because the construction process back then was ongoing, there might be a warehouse still intact that stored useable, undamaged panels and equipment. They found a building on the outskirts of the little town and most of the materials inside were unscathed.

Darin and Josh had borrowed a near new Peterbilt semi-tractor and a flat bed trailer that was parked inside the brick mechanics shop of the Beales Pipeline Company. They loaded and hauled what they needed back to their newly expanding town. An abundance of free material, supplies and equipment for any and all projects the men could possibly dream of was easily at their disposal. Finding it and moving it back to their location was the only cost in sweat labor. They estimated the potential cost savings to be near two-hundred-thousand dollars.

The dedicated power grid should accommodate any anticipated electrical needs a small community would require. It will be nice not to have to rely on generators and the underground hydro-electric system anymore other than for backup purposes.

Several small families and a few young couples had moved from Norad Mountain Sanctuary. They made New Elmar their new home. Darin was grateful for the help and socialization. One family happened to have two young boys about the same age as Annie and Emma. He recognized the testosterone levels all increased when the boys were introduced to his girls. Positive attractions caused him some alarm. The four young adventurers were often nowhere to be found nor did they always stay within ear shot of the bunker.

"Hatty, any idea where the girls are this time?" Darin asked expecting to hear a no answer.

"No, I haven't seen them since breakfast and the Challenger's gone so who knows where they might be. It's not like them not to tell us where they are going. Now you have me a little worried too, Darin."

"Josh, Penny, did the girls happen to tell you where they were going this morning?"

Penny answered. "Yeah, Emma said she and Annie and the Stratford boys were going to go hangout at your old house."

Darin looked at Hatty and raised his eyebrows, knowing what types of mischief they could be getting into.

Hatty recognized the look and spoke. "We need to trust them, Darin."

"I know, but it's hard. They're all still just kids. I know what was on my mind back then."

"You have to trust them or it will just drive you crazy." Hatty smiled.

"Maybe we need to talk to Mike and Mary and see what they think?"

Well, that will be an uncomfortable conversation, but, yeah, let's do that before we talk with the girls."

"I'll have a conversation with the girls when the time is right, just the three of us, if that's okay with you." Hatty nodded, more than willing to stay clear of this heavy parental responsibility.

Darin's thoughts drifted to his son, Abe, wondering where he was and what he was doing at that moment. He was so happy to see him at Reese and Karla's wedding. Being away from home, he had matured so fast. A conversation like this would have been so much easier with him, instead of the girls. "I wonder how Abe is doing?" he asked.

Hatty recognized her husband was having one of those moments that only a hug could reassure. "Everything's going to be alright, Honey. Besides, now that my dad is like almost the new President of Federation Earth." She laughed in awkward disbelief, trying to help lighten up the moment for Darin.

"I think I need a 'Sun Drop,' I'm really thirsty." He pulled the ice-cold bottle out of the cooler and removed the bottle cap with the opener on the handle.

"Everything's going to be okay, Honey." Hatty, gave Darin a quirky smile and headed toward the bunker entrance.

THE GAPERS VIEW

Day 581, March 11th, 2028

St. Thomas, British Virgin Islands

"Yes, please bring us two blended margaritas and a shrimp cocktail appetizer, thank you." The retired president opened his menu and began perusing the entrée dinner options. "What are you hungry for tonight, Maggie?"

"I think I'd like to try some fish. I've never had Dolphin Fish or Tarpon, have you, Mitch?"

"Actually, no I never have either. How about if you get one and I'll get the other and we can share and try them both."

"This is exciting. I think I could get used to this retirement stuff." Maggie chuckled as she dipped one of the jumbo shrimps into the cocktail sauce and took a big bite. She made a sound of approval and encouraged her husband to join her in the celebration.

They shared their meals together and Mitch decided to present a toast. "Mrs. Baylor, here's to wonderful days together where from now on our lives may always be like a honeymoon." They tapped their margarita glasses together and both took multiple sips off of the salt coated rims. In all of the emotions of the celebration, neither person thought the margaritas might be made with strawberries. Mitch Baylor started to gasp for air as his wind pipe instantly began to swell shut. He clenched his throat with a look of horror on his face that Maggie hadn't experienced for many years, usually they were more careful but in the moment they both had let their guards down for their personal safety.

"Oh my God, Mitch, I left the epi-pen in the room." Maggie began to panic and got up from her chair and yelled. "Does anyone have an epi-pen? Someone please, help me. My husband is having an allergic reaction to strawberries."

The maître d' called over a loudspeaker for the hotels house doctor to come to the dining hall. Maggie explained to the doctor what happened and asked if he had an epi-pen. He opened an old-fashioned medical bag and pulled one out. Holding it on Mitch's thigh he injected the epinephrine and almost instantly the anaphylactic reaction subsided.

Mitch started to breath normally again and the color in his face and hands got lighter. "Wow, that was a close one, Maggie. Thank you, Doctor."

Maggie began to cry, "geez, I almost killed you!"

"I'm okay, Honey. I've relied on you for so long to take care of me, it's not your fault, Maggie. I need to start carrying an Epi-pen around myself from now on. I shouldn't place that responsibility on anyone other than myself. I'm sorry, it was pretty selfish of me."

"I never thought to ask if the margaritas had strawberries in them."

The maître d' interrupted. "Madam, these margaritas are made with pink grapefruit, no strawberries."

The couple looked at each other and then down to the scattered fragments of dolphin fish and tarpon left randomly in disarray over their dinner plates.

"Well, I guess I won't be having ocean fish anymore." The off comment struck the couples funny and out of discomfort it became contagious. The gapers view slowly paid less attention to the unannounced emergency disturbance and continued finishing their dinners.

"May we have the check, please." Mitch Baylor took a drink from his water glass and apologized once more to Maggie for his carelessness. "I'm sorry, Maggie. That kind of ruined a good day for us."

"Mitch, how would you have known the fish was going to do that to you? Are their any other food items we should be concerned about?"

"Not that I am aware of. I did hear about a blood test that can be analyzed using artificial intelligence, they have been able to isolate specific bacteria that helps our bodies function better, determining which bacteria is missing from my body and which types I have that are bad for me. I read that they can correlate it to which foods shouldn't be eaten."

Maggie shook her head, "Just imagine what the future will be like in twenty years with all the new technology. I hope the world can figure out how to quit killing each other."

Mitch Baylor paused and reflected for a moment, thinking about the plans that have been in place. "Yeah, me too. Would you like to go for a walk around the city, Maggie?"

"Okay, I grabbed a map at the front desk while you checked in yesterday. It showed the best walking routes along the coastline through the city. We can find a nice place to sit and watch the sunset, but let's go up to the room first and change into more comfortable walking clothes and shoes."

"We might not get out of the room before dark." Mitch winked and smiled.

"Does the epinephrine do the same thing as those little blue pills?" They both laughed and made their way to the elevator.

****

"I'm a bit surprised about Elan's decision. Have you been able to talk to John and Ace since our official retirement dates?"

"Actually, yes, we met together one last time before we

left Norad and discussed who might be good replacements as Governors of the Mid-West and Southwestern states."

"Who did you decide on?"

"We all agreed on Alphonsa Orlov, as a replacement for Ace."

"Really?"

"You don't agree?"

"I'm not sure. He and his group had a rocky start with Karla and Reese and even with Major Baker and his crew. What changed your mind about him?"

"We all discussed it at great length. It was Ace's comments that caused Elan and I to judge him differently. He and Ailyn and Reese stopped at Alphonsa's encampment and spent some quality time there before traveling back to their home at Norad Mountain. I trust Ace's intuition and his established trust with the group. It sounded like Alphonsa was more concerned about me screwing it all up then who was placed into new positions of power and control. He wants worldwide peace just like us. A different stance than what we had been used to dealing with in Russian history. President Palarov gave me a full endorsement of the man's credentials and vouches for his integrity as a man of his word. It was a unanimous decision to let Alphonsa serve and show his allegiance for re-building."

"Well, I trust your intuition and I hope it all works out in the end."

"Wow, look at that sunset." Mitch Baylor put his arm around his young spouse and kissed her on the cheek. "Could it get any better than this, Maggie?"

"Oh, I don't know, maybe when we get back to our room." Maggie gave him a mischievous smile and snuggled in tighter to her man.

DIVINE INTERVENTION

Day 595, March 25th, 2028

Ely, Nevada

John and Matt Cartwright sat together in front of their campfire talking about past memories. It was making them both feel happy and terribly sad at the same time. The loss of John's wife Barbara, Matt's mother, would always be the toughest memory the two men would endure. They both missed her terribly. Always a smile every morning, even at the end. Standing in her kitchen, coffee in one hand and a cigarette in the other. Neither of them could say or do enough to convince her to give up the cancer sticks. She loved smoking all the way till the end, then professed wishing she would have listened to her men. She died a horrible death. No treatments available. No real pain management to speak of. John convinced her to take as many cannabis gummies as she wanted, hating to see her in such pain. They seemed to take the edge off a little until the last day. It was unbearable for all of them.

John had been a man of faith for most of his life. He often told stories of divine intervention while serving and fighting in the Iraq war and Afghanistan. Angels, he'd say. I've got angels. Experiencing his wife's pain shook his belief system to the core. The God he had served so faithfully seemed to have abandoned him and his family when he needed Him the most. How could the Healer, his Lord and Savior allow such heartache and pain. He found himself cursing the whole concept of an omnificent being, until one night after the world came to an abrupt stop, he was watching his son sleeping in the cave, the pale moonlights reflection shining into the entranceway. It reminded him of when Matt was first born and all of the complications during Barbara's labor. The doctor's facial expressions and demeanor weren't very optimistic. John silently made a deal with God that if he saved his son, he would serve Him and the needs of others for the rest of his life on earth. He was a man of integrity and when John Cartwright makes a promise, he keeps it.

Maybe a man only get's one of these saving grace opportunities in life, blaming himself for his wife's death, but then accepting the realization that it was the chemicals inhaled from her smoking. It was her choice, the black death, hard to deny it. Smoking stole his precious Barbara way earlier than both had expected. They should have grown old together. "Have you had enough to eat, Matt?"

"Yeah, I think so, Dad, thanks."

"I'll take care of cleaning up tonight; do you have anything else you'd like to do?" Since becoming a new town, several new people and families decided to take up residence around their domed bunker home. Ely, Nevada was starting over in a different location just outside of the old town line. There were several young people around Matt's age, which he had met and was getting to know better each day, but he hadn't allowed himself the luxury of friendship yet. Maybe it was his introverted personality. He felt more comfortable hanging out with his dad. Maybe time would change this, or maybe one of the girls would. "Why don't you go hang out with your new friends, they have to be more fun than being with your boring dad."

"I like hanging with you, Dad, besides, I could say the same thing to you."

"I've got an idea. How about we throw a party. A potluck that will give everyone a better chance to get to know each other like neighbors."

"That's a great idea, Dad. We can all have food cubes and water and talk about the good old days."

John knew from his tone that he was trying to be funny. He thought, *at least he hasn't totally lost his sense of humor.* "Let's plan on going out on a scavenge trip early tomorrow morning before it gets to hot. We can try to find party food, then cook up a bunch of hamburgers from the meat Elan delivered to us last month."

"I'm hungry for chocolate cake and chocolate frosting. Maybe we can find a bunch of box cake mixes."

John spent the next hour cleaning up the dishes and doing the daily housekeeping chores. Matt took some time to stack a full cord of wood they found along side a garage about a mile from home. When they were done both were ready to call it a night.

"Night, Dad. See you in the morning."

"Good night, Son. Sweet sleep, buddy."

****

The morning sun was just starting to share its first light from the eastern horizon. A full moon created luminescent light in direct competition. Not a cloud in the sky as was pretty typical for this time of the year in Nevada.

"Matt, come on Buddy, time to get up and get going." John put together a small soft plastic cooler with snacks and water bottles. They found some boxes of powdered drink packets that helped give them some flavor variety. They both liked the lemonade mix the best.

Bug-out bags and rifles in hand, they walked toward the

rock crawler. Unfortunately starting the machine this early was going to wake up the entire town, but it couldn't be helped. The end goal had priority. The desert was an unforgiving place. Certain vehicles worked better than others. The crawler never left them stranded or ever got stuck. After Matt's climbing experience with the members of the Rover team, there was no obstacle he felt uncomfortable maneuvering up, on, or over.

Matt shifted into first gear and idled down the worn path. When he felt that they were far enough away from town he put the foot pedal down and it forced them both back against their seats. The raw power was electrifying this early in the morning. It created a sense of exhilaration that was rare in their new existence. The forced desert air was still fairly cool and the generated wind blew their hair backwards. They both needed haircuts.

Before John had joined the Marine Corp, he had long hair. Over the last two years it was long enough to place back into a ponytail again, different from his military haircut so easily achievable with electricity and a local barbershop. Matt just let his fly free. Both of them had raccoon eye tans from constantly wearing sunglasses. John thought maybe before the party they could spend a little more time on personal hygiene. They had lost some of the daily habits taken for granted in a fully operational society.

Ely, Nevada itself was pretty picked through from the southside, toward the north. Scavenging became routine and helped pass the time. Matt seemed to like it more than his dad. It was like a non-stop rummage sale. Two outlying subdivisions just outside of the city were left until last. There were upper middle-class cookie-cutter homes all tightly built in rows that lined the city blocks. Hundreds of homes that shared similar design but each had different colored siding and shingles. No way either man would ever live in this type of urban sprawl as the open air feeling of their family's ranch better served their needs. Door to door reconnaissance was certainly going to reap rewards though. Skirting past a tattered sign

'Roche-Del-Rio' marked the entrance of the subdivision, several cars were piled up blocking easy access. Matt jumped up on the curb and motored over a dirty picket fence and a dried dead row of hedges. Once past the vehicle obstacles, they jumped off the curb back onto the road.

"Geez, Dad, why don't we just move into one of these?" Matt's said sarcastically.

"Cause there's no place like home, Son." They both laughed out loud and parked in the middle of the first block and shut down the motor. "Let's start with this one first and work our way around the block."

The sidewalk was unmaintained and the front windows were all dirty. John looked inside to what seemed like a living room that hadn't been cleaned in forever and yet everything was neatly in its proper place.

"Is the door unlocked?" Matt reached for the door lever.

"I'll break through the window and unlock the door for you." John carefully removed any glass from the frame that could cut him. He straddled the frame and went out of sight for a few seconds. The door opened and Matt joined his dad inside. No footprints on the dusty floor told both of them the house was uninhabited, at least by the living, although neither of them could smell any decomposition. Maybe the owners tried to bug-out upon hearing an emergency siren or reading a news clip on their phones.

Pictures on the wall next to a baby grand piano showed several photos of a family of four, two adult males with two small children possibly pre-kindergarten age. They looked like siblings who were from different cultural birth parents, maybe of Spanish descent.

"I think the house was empty when the shit hit the fan, Dad."

"Yeah, I think you're right. Let's stay together though, okay. How about we start in the kitchen."

John pushed through two swinging café doors and noticed a taller set of matching white cabinets that looked built in underneath a staircase. He opened the hinged doors and discovered a pantry just packed full of canned goods and other variety staple foods. "Go get the totes from the crawler, Matt. I don't think we will have to look through any other houses today. We can coordinate with the others to scavenge the rest of the homes and bring a bigger vehicle to haul it all in."

They spent about an hour sorting through the various foods, looking at all of the expiration dates. They filled two totes with enough for the celebration party. This family seemed like they were planning for birthday parties.

Day 602, April 1st, 2028
New Ely, Nevada

Including the Cartwrights, there were twelve residents who were making New Ely, Nevada their home. They were all busy making preparations for a family style get-together. A new package of three white plastic table cloths was discovered while the group made house-by-house searches for food and valuables. Decorative flower-patterned paper plates and clear plastic throw away utensils were placed into twelve settings along with twelve plastic red solo cups and matching red paper napkins.

John and Matt were now clean shaven and both had spent some time making themselves more presentable. They were in charge of grilling the hamburger patties on a steel grid that layed over the edge of a steel wheel fire ring. The rest of the group was busy preparing the rest of the meal. Chips which even after two years were still crunchy, sealed inside their air tight cellophane bags. Five different kinds of jarred pickles and Bush's Original Baked beans, which were the most abundant canned good found in nearly every home searched.

The event was taking shape and spirits were high. All of them hoped this would bring them more together as friends and as a team, more than just casual neighbors.

"Would anyone like to say something before we eat?" John asked politely.

"I will, John," said, Julie Abrams, a middle-aged-strong minded woman who had spent most of her adult life in service to the country on the backend of the government. She had been responsible for developing some of the hybrid seed production used deep below the surface of Norad Mountain, and now around the country.

John felt a slight attraction to her, but hadn't come forward to share this with anyone yet. He wouldn't need to, for he had no poker face. Matt recognized the attraction right away.

"Thanks, Julie, yes please do."

"Well, this is a real treat for us all, isn't it? Coming together gives us a chance to create connection and community. I hope we can allow ourselves the freedom to open up our hearts and minds to each other. We have a lot of work to do together in the upcoming years. I'm so happy to have another chance to be a part of such a great cause again and I'm even happier it's here with all of you. Thank you to John and Matt for paving the way forward for us and for finding all this great food for us to enjoy together. Let's eat!"

Everyone agreed and the bowls of food started to be passed around the table.

'I AM'

Day 635, May 4th, 2028

Barre Mills, Wisconsin

The cabin's interior looked like it had been ransacked by looters. Furniture was tipped over and lay spread out in disarray across the floor. Out near the well pump, the rusty handle was stuck in the upward position. The white porcelain pitcher sitting on its side apart from its matching basin that a day ago was flung full force into the oval mirror above the antique dresser. A dented lone canned good with no label had been rolled across the laminate flooring and rested against a pile of dirty clothes along side of Jake's small caliber pistol with an empty chamber.

Several clear empty liquor bottles were stacked indiscriminately around the cabin floor. Only to a non-alcoholic would it appear as a lifetime of consumption. To those who'd know from experience, it was only a few months' worth.

The distress was evident. Unorganized housekeeping alone was evidence of embraced alcoholic demons and disease. So much loss and despair. Too many unresolved issues burdening one man's soul.

Survivors guilt, unmatched by the inexperienced. *Why did they all have to die and I didn't? Am I in hell? Is this my punishment for not confessing all of my sins?*

Jake's mind came in and out of wakeful consciousness. An empty bottle of Lilly Darvon, child proof cap twisted off, laying empty on the floor next to his right leg. The pain and confusion obviously was simply too much for him to cope with.

His will to live on had all but disappeared now. There was

no more questioning. Even with the proper care of a medical facility, the damage was done. The chemical composition of the pills and alcohol in Jake's bloodstream would have made it impossible for him to survive without a full life support system.

He thought to himself, *I can hear my heart beat.* Lub-dub, lub-dub, lub. Pure light everywhere.

"You now have a choice to make, Jake. All you have to do is confess with your mouth and believe in your heart that,
'I Am.'

Jakes life passed in front of his eyes in a fraction of a millisecond. He began to cry and then there was nothing. Total blackness.

FAKE WINDOWS

Day 640, May 9, 2028

Mauston, Wisconsin

Mauston, Wisconsin had kept Brad and Paula properly sustained, but they were running dangerously low on useable foods marked within the manufacturer's suggested expiration dates. To eat food that would get them sick now would prove catastrophic.

Attempts at gardening outside had failed, the soil was just too acidic with the arid soil conditions, but they did manage to build a small greenhouse from a DIY kit they found at the local hardware store. A barn that suffered minimal damage had some composted cow manure which provided fertile soil for the plastic trays and bins that came inside the kit. Seed packets of radishes, lettuce, kale, green beans, peas, and tomatoes were all starting to sprout, but it would be a while before they could enjoy a harvest.

"We should be able to start eating fresh lettuce and radishes soon, Paula."

"I can't wait, eating all those canned vegetables is getting a little old. To have fresh from the garden will be way better. I'm not sure if we can keep going without real protein though. We don't have any animals to raise like we had on the farm. Maybe we should have accepted Major Baker's help? Can we call out on that radio he left us and see if they answer?"

Brad answered. "He said it only has a range of about ten miles. I doubt if it would do any good. We could go to the Benson's and see if we can figure out how to get their Ham radio to work."

"Can we go now Brad, no offense but I need to have some people contact, don't you?" Paula had been getting steadily more depressed every day. The ups and downs of survival living were starting to wear on her mentally. He too, admitted yearning for social contact and a greater purpose.

The old 1985 Chevrolet pickup truck started right up. It was Brad's baby since getting his license in 2003, his sophomore year in high school. The four-wheel drive had come in handy several times traversing different road conditions they encountered while collecting and scavenging.

"I only met Jack and Sally a couple of times. Did you know them pretty well, Brad?"

"Yeah, he was a member of the fire department with my dad. I never have been in their house though. Hopefully the radio equipment still works." Brad had installed a brand-new commercial combination diesel welder/generator that you would normally see in the back of a construction foreman's company pickup truck. It came in handy several times to power tools and equipment that they used to break into commercial buildings with.

The Benson homestead sat in the middle of one hundred

acres of hardwoods with a small pond on the left side of the driveway that was fed by a narrow brook that flowed in from backwaters of the Lemonwier River. It was discolored and looked dead from above. The mature trees and the contour of the landscape provided natural wind break protection. The antennas looked damaged. Some were bent sideways and busted at their bases.

"We'll figure it out, Paula." He could see his wife's countenance changed the closer they drove toward the house. Brad had limited electrical experience, just enough to be dangerous. "Hopefully we can find some instruction manuals." He knew the radio might have specific power requirements to operate with his generator as a power source.

"I'm glad you know what you're doing, because I don't have a clue about anything with electronics."

"Hopefully, I know just enough not to electrocute myself." Brad laughed and saw Paula wasn't easily amused.

The four-wheel drive came in handy again, maneuvering over some brush and a smaller tree trunk that had fallen in front of the house. The metal buildings looked intact, except for a smaller one that had a larger uprooted tree that fell onto its roof.

Brad parked and Paula stepped out first and walked around the hood of their truck. She met Brad at his driver's side door and grabbed the back pack he was handing to her, along with a small rifle she slung over her shoulders. "Do you think we'll find the Bensons inside the house?"

Brad closed the door and as he was putting his pack on and shouldering his rifle, said, "I hope not." Paula had seen Brad's facial expression hundred of times when encountering decaying bodies.

A very low decibel humming vibration was causing the hair to tickle on the back of Paula's hands. She pulled her 380 ACP out from behind her back and held it at the ready position. She felt like she was being watched, yet no one was alive much less anywhere in sight.

Brad noticed her sudden change in posture and asked,

"What is it?"

"Do you feel that?"

"No what?"

"It feels like we're being watched."

"Really, honey? There's nobody left alive anywhere in Mauston."

A voice came from out of nowhere. "Are you sure about that, Brad Pintar?"

Brad and Paula nearly jumped out of their skins, the sudden sound of talking surprised them like never before.

"Who's there, come out where I can see you." Brad and Paula both took cover behind their truck bed and had their guns rested against the truck box.

"Brad it's me Jack, and Sally's with me too. We are underground in a bunker under the basement. Look at the front porch. See the camera monitor and speaker underneath in the corner?"

"Oh my God, you guys are alive? I didn't know you had a bunker, Jack. Have you been down there since the bombs hit?"

"Yes, we weren't sure it was safe. You're the first living things we've seen on the cameras. We'll be right up, give us a minute."

The thought of survivors gave Paula a total transformation in demeanor. Compared to Brad, she was desperate for human contact. Ever since hugging that Hatty woman with Nolan Baker and his crew, she missed thriving with living human connections. Constant contact with the dead and decaying was like performing an acting part in a horror movie. Paula hated horror movies.

Jack and Sally emerged from a sealed hidden Murphy Door they had built into the foundation wall of their home's basement. They walked up the basement steps into the kitchen and then into their living room to the front entrance door. Their eyes squinted from the natural light of the sun that they had learned to live without for the last two years.

"Hi Brad, hi Paula." Jack approached the familiar couple,

reaching out his hand. Sally hugged Paula, and the two women began shedding tears of joy. Discovering each other alive, after surviving such chaotic circumstances. It was quite overwhelming even for Brad and Jack.

"Have you called out on your radio equipment, Jack?"

"I never hooked it up inside the bunker. My power source was used only for bare necessities and I didn't feel comfortable coming outside until seeing you guys. The last transmission I heard was that President Baylor was held up safe in Norad Mountain. After the grid went down and hearing that nukes had been used on the east coast, we went underground and locked the door in case they dropped any in Wisconsin. About a week later we watched the winds and fires blow past our camera. I couldn't believe the camera made it through undamaged and still worked for us. It didn't take us long to just stop watching, it was too depressing, until about a year ago. I wanted to see if the sun had come out again. To our surprise it had. Then we saw it rain. We wondered if we were the only people alive and then started a daily routine of checking the weather and keeping a log. I had just turned on the camera today at my usual time and to our surprise saw you coming up the driveway toward the house." Jack wiped a tear from his eye. The raw emotions were felt all around.

The two couples spent the rest of the afternoon walking around the Bensons property, assessing the damage to the radio antennas, while Paula jotted down needed supplies that they could go retrieve to put the system back on the mend. Brad and Paula took turns filling in the absent details of their experiences for the Bensons.

"Would you guys share a meal with us, are you hungry?" Sally asked.

The two couples entered the house and walked down the basement steps, then again down the twenty steps into the underground bunker. The Murphy Door was left open this time. A secondary entrance door opened with a gentle push; it led them into a breezeway with storage shelves partially empty of survival goods. Jack opened a third door allowing them into a mechanical room that held the hydro electric generator and water heater and air filtration system. Brad smelled the pungent odor from a waste system that broke down all organic materials. It was a pretty efficient system compared to his own and now he knew how the Bensons were able to comfortably stay underground for so long. The main living area was a twenty by forty-foot rectangle. The open concept provided basic creature comforts for two survivors. There were three doors, one on each wall that provided extra storage for food and supplies. Glued on the face of each of the doors were three different bright pictures of realistic landscapes you would see out each door's direction on a sunny day as if looking out a window of the main house. Curtains hung down from rods, tied back to give a realistic dimensional illusion. Paula was mesmerized and wished she had thought of such a simple familiarity feature. Knowing they were fake windows would take special effort to summon strong imaginations.

"Wow, you guys really did it up right, Jack," Brad said with jealous enthusiasm.

"Yeah, the hardest part was building it so no one knew we were building it." Jack replied. "It took us four years to complete, we started back in 2020." Brad nodded his head, knowing what the political climate was like back then.

"Where did you guys stay over the last two years?" Sally asked.

"We have a bunker too. It's about half this size though." Brad did the best he could to explain. "Last year, we stepped out of our bunker for the first time because we were running out of food. Everything looked burnt and was covered with ash but the air was breathable so we started scavenging through houses. We checked out the Quick Trip store and thought maybe we would get lucky. When we came outside again, we came face to face with a strange looking military vehicle speaking to us over a loudspeaker. There were eight people onboard, six were military, and a woman about our age and her step son. They startled us and we shot at them. Luckily our bullets ricocheted off the windshield and after everybody calmed down, we managed to have a civil conversation. They were on their way to see the woman's parents who survived in a bunker up near La Crosse." Jack and Sally listened attentively to the remarkable story.

Brad continued. "They wanted us to establish an outpost in Mauston that would allow travelers a resting spot. They gave us a shortwave handheld radio to make contact with them when they came back through Mauston the next day. Paula and I decided that night we didn't want to run an outpost and that we would rather just be left alone, not thinking at the time that someday food and supplies were going to become harder to find and to be totally honest, we missed not having people around us. That's why we are here. We thought we could make contact with your radio. The last words we had with Sergeant Major Baker was that most of the deep southern states weathered the chaos and the country was trying to re-establish again. If we changed our minds, we were to ask specifically for him by radio and he was willing to help us. We're ready to ask for his help and yours too. Will you guys help us make contact with your radio?"

****

Brad and Jack drove into the city together, heading to the hardware store to collect all the materials and supplies they needed to repair the broken antennas. They spent a good part of the day completing the repairs and now were ready to hook up the power to Brad's generator in his truck.

"Let's do one more check to make sure we didn't miss anything, Jack."

"Will the power converter regulate the current properly so we don't blow anything out on the radio?" Jack was equally concerned about the alternative power source working effectively.

"I think the worst that could happen is we blow a fuse." Brad touched the link on the backside of the radio receiver. Are we ready? I'll go fire up the generator. Turn on the radio after you hear it idle down Jack."

The diesel engine smoked a little upon starting but then the air cleared and the motor slowly gained in RPM's and then changed down to its normal running idle speed. Jack flipped the switch on and a red indicator light showed evidence that it was powered up. Brad walked in from the front porch and heard a soft humming static sound emitting from the desk top speakers. Jack turned the volume up a little and began scanning his normal frequencies that he enjoyed monitoring as an amateur operator. None of the familiar stops had any sound other than radio static.

34.90mhz was the emergency National Guard frequency and he hoped it would provide him with proof of existence still available in America. Hitting the mic for the first time since 2026, Jack spoke his call sign. "Wisconsin 363543 to any available responder, come in please. This is Jack Benson from Mauston Wisconsin, come in please, over."

Norad Mountain operators were trained to detect and respond to all and any transmissions. Specialist O'Neil recognized this as a new call sign and immediately responded. "WI363543, this is Norad Mountain Sanctuary, Specialist O'Neil responding back to you, I have received your transmission, over."

"Hello, wow it is so good to hear another voice again. My wife Sally and I just came out of our underground bunker today, and we are with one other couple, Brad and Paula Pintar who met Sergeant Major Nolan Baker and his crew about a year after the power went down. It's a long story, but they were told to contact him. Is that possible?"

"Yes, it is possible, Mr. Benson. I believe Major Baker and his crew are currently operating in South Carolina. I will make contact with him and connect us, hold on for me please."

Jack waited patiently at the mic, while Sally and Brad and Paula paced behind him showing natural signs of excitement.

"Mr. Benson, I'll patch you through to Major Baker, now.

Go ahead Sir."

"Major Baker, this is Jack Benson another survivor from Mauston Wisconsin. Do you remember an encounter with Brad and Paula Pintar? They are here with me right now."

"Yes sir, please put them on." Nolan replied with his crew attentively listening behind him.

"Hello, Major Baker, it's Brad Pintar, you said if we ever changed our minds to reach out to you."

"Yes, I'm happy you did, Brad. Is everything okay? Are you and Paula alright?"

"Paula and I made a huge selfish mistake by not accepting your help and not being willing to open an outpost, we hope you can forgive us again." The couple stood tightly together, Paula's head dropped down and rested against Brads left shoulder. The emotions were running high. Jack and Sally decided to give them some space and stepped out onto the front porch again for privacy. It appeared there was some unfinished business to attend to between the communicating parties.

"How is Hatty?" Paula asked.

"I haven't seen them for awhile now, but no news is good news. A lot has happened since we met. I'm sure none of you are aware of what's transpired over the last year. You'll need to catch up on what's all taken place."

"Major, we really miss being with people and it's gotten harder to find food that is safe." Paula changed the subject feeling the need to provide him with an honest appraisal of their situation.

"How did you find the Bensons?"

"They had the ham radio equipment. We went to their house and discovered that they had also built an underground bunker. It's really a miracle any of us are still alive. Where are you now Major Baker?"

"Currently, we are in South Carolina, my crew is almost finished setting up another outpost, then we were planning on circling back to Darin and Hatty Knox's outpost. We could plan on stopping at your location again on the way through. Would that be alright?"

"When would you arrive?

"It will take us about a week."

"That would be great. Do you still need another outpost in our city?"

"Yes, it would be very helpful, especially now that there are four of you there. I'll contact Elan Must and coordinate a helicopter drop of supplies and materials. Are the Benson's on board with this?" Major Baker could hear Paula ask their permission as she must have pressed the mic button at the same time.

"They are both just as excited as Brad and I are."

"Great, so are we. I'll reach out to Hatty and tell her the news. See you all in a week. Rover IV signing off.

Day 648, May 16, 2028
Mauston, Wisconsin

The Rover and Darin's grey Dodge Ram Power Wagon pulled up to the I-94 bridge overpass. Brad and Paula were sitting on the Chevy's tailgate, they stood up together when the vehicles came to a stop.

The Rover's cargo door lowered to the ground and Major Nolan Baker stepped out and approached the smiling couple. Darin and Hatty were already making their way over to greet Brad and Paula. They decided this reunion was too important to miss out on and Hatty was sure she and her husband could be of service helping everyone feel more comfortable about the future.

"Hi Paula." Hatty went right in for a warm embrace, while Darin introduced himself to Brad with a more casual handshake greeting. The Rover crew stayed inside preparing an unloading plan when they arrive at the Pintars building location.

Major Baker extended his outstretched hand first to Brad and then to Paula. "It's so good to see you guys again. How about we get right to work. We can follow you to where your new outpost can be constructed and off load some needed supplies and materials."

Brad remembered the last interaction they shared with Nolan and felt strong emotions receiving second chances. "Okay, follow us then."

The three vehicles turned around and drove back down Hwy 82 away from the freeway interchange. The first road left took them past an empty Fed-Ex distribution center and then past a Redi-mix plant. Hatty noticed the name on the plywood sign at the driveway. It was her dad's employer's plant in Mauston. She didn't realize they had one there and couldn't wait to let him know she passed it.

When they arrived minutes later at Brad and Paula's bunker site, the crew began offloading the glass panels manufactured underneath the Rovers underbelly. Brad and Paula worked with Hatty and the others to organize the surplus foods being left for their consumption. To their dismay they were shone how to operate their new space age food synthesizer and like everyone is at first, they were amazed at the new technology.

Over the course of an hour, Hatty tried her best to bring the survivors up to speed on what all transpired over the last two years… "and that's how John Pillsbury and my father became the new leaders of Federation Earth."

"So, every surviving country is working together in agreement now? No more power struggles over money and power? We all work together to live as one?" Sally couldn't believe it. It all sounded too good to be true.

"With no monetary system, everybody works for the benefit of others instead of themselves. No more poverty or famine. Every country has its strengths and weaknesses. They produce and give from the focused strengths of their group labor. Their needs are met in trade from every other country's collaborated effort."

"Who's responsible for this new idea?"

"That's funny you ask," said Hatty. "I don't really know.

My dad never told me that."

WARP SPEED

Day 650, May 18th, 2028

Norad Mountain Sanctuary

In the last two years, several hundred survivors were brought into the fold and were brought up to date on the countries planning and recent history. It was a true testament of the resilience of these individuals. The will to live is stronger than the idea of failure. These folks all had beaten unsurmountable odds by simply not being blind deniers. Their planning and eyes for detail placed them in a minute percentage of the former population class caught in the catastrophic pathway of nuclear death and destruction. They had cheated death when it knocked on their bunker's door.

Specialist O'Neil along with a few other Norad radio operators were granted the blessing of first contact. Hearing the sounds of new voices, searching for anyone still alive gave them all a new sense of hope.

Ambassador Ayer, sat in his new office behind a

hardwood desk instead of the steering wheel of his 2024 Freightliner semi-truck. His overused coffee mug showed a picture of Captain James T. Kirk and his first mate Spock with the words 'Warp Speed' displayed on the side. He had taken it with him from inside his battered home on a former visit. It seemed like just yesterday that he waited for his Ailyn to arrive safely, unsure if she would, the emotions running so high. In his wildest dreams, he would have never thought the events of the last two years would have occurred in his lifetime.

He dozed off and found himself face to face with Regina Putman sitting provocatively next to a man he assumed could only be Lucifer himself. They looked at each other and smiled and then both started to laugh out loud. It was thunderous. Ace placed his hands over his ears as the sound was deafening and caused blood to start flowing slowly out of his eardrums. The pain was anguishing and intolerable. *This isn't real, it's all just a dream,* he heard the words spoken from deep inside his long-tormented soul. Darkness, light, back to darkness, Ace then found himself lying on his back in an aromatic field of wild flowers. A bumble bee flew in front of his face and stopped. Looking deep into its dark eyes his hands were being changed into smoke and they began to be sucked into the darkness until he no longer existed in the field but could now see through the eyes of the flying bee. He flew through a broken window of a familiar building. It was the assisted living complex his mother had moved to in her last years. The hallway was collapsed in on itself. Broken remnants of cheery pictures lay off level on the darkened walls. Room numbers visually passed by, 329, 330, 331, 332 and 333, his mother's room. The door was open and a young woman no more than twenty sat upright in a chair facing the broken-out window. She turned sideways and Ace recognized the young woman. It was his mother. *How is this possible,* he thought to himself. "Mom?" the word sounded spoken. "Is that really you?" He asked, unsure what to think.

"It is me, Daniel. I need your help. You need to help get me to your father through this." The young woman held up an antique hairbrush. "Come find me, Daniel. Find me and help me get to your father."

"I will, Mom." Ace woke up and wiped his eyes free of the catnap's tensions. He knew what he needed to do next and called out to Specialist O'Neil for help.

"What can I do for you, Sir?"

"I need to go see my daughter and son-in-law in Wisconsin, can you help me accomplish this as soon as possible?"

"Yes, Sir. Will Mrs. Ayer be traveling with you too, or anyone else?"

"Yes, she and my son and daughter-in-law also if they aren't too busy."

"I'll make the arrangements, Sir."

"Thank you, Mr. O'Neil. Have I told you lately how much I appreciate all your help and how great you are at your job?"

"Yesterday, Sir. Thank you, I appreciate it very much."

Day 651, May 19, 2028
New Elmar, Wisconsin

"I want to stay here with Hatty and Darin and the girls." Ailyn wanted to spend as much time as possible with her family as chances to do so were lessened with her husband's new position of leadership.

"Okay, we won't be gone long, I have to do this, honey, thanks for understanding and not asking too many questions." Ace kissed Ailyn goodbye and he and Reese and Karla stepped inside the chopper and the door closed behind them.

******

Setting down onto the 'Guest A' parking area of the assisted living facility was smooth as always. Ace's pilot was very capable with former military and commercial experience after retiring from the service.

A white LLV was parked in the far corner of the lot. The sign on its side read, 'TYVEK MAINTENANCE SERVICES.' Ace wondered if the driver was a visitor or just caught in the wrong place at the right time.

A team of four, fully armed, Karla at point, with the pilot covering the groups six entered the front entrance and Ace motioned directions with his hand toward the stairwell door. It was clear of bodies all the way up to the third floor. Karla swung the door open and all of them instantly saw that the hallway was not empty. Bodies lay scattered randomly around the nurse's station along with walkers and wheelchairs. Bodies that after two years had become dried up and mummified. Witnessing gruesome decomposition processes in mass will never be accepted by the living. Some of the bed ridden inhabitants could be seen as the group walked down the hallway past the room numbers from Ace's dream. Then they arrived at his mother's old room. He felt it ironic that the room shared the same familiarity as his alarm clocks time on day one. Was there hidden meaning or was this just another coincidence?

His mom had left him a few years earlier. Spared from the agonizing death experienced by the other residents. The pull to revisit her old room was strong. He knew from his dream what to look for. Was the brush symbolism? How could such an inanimate object hold his mother's soul in place, capturing and preventing her accension into her afterlife? Ace didn't understand, but he would be obedient, as nothing would stop him from completing this last task of love.

Ace entered the doorway and immediately saw the rooms inhabitant spread out on the floor beside her bed. He quickly covered the body with a blanket and then entered the bathroom. A vanity table and single chair rested against the open wall. It was there. A brush Ace recognized. Maybe it was left behind, or maybe this woman had stolen it? Ace sensed a strong intuition. *Was this your brush Mom?* He asked silently in his mind.

When he picked up the brush, Reese and Karla witnessed Ace's eyes blinking rapidly. He fell backwards to the floor and began to shake violently just like his experience at Mike and Sue's bunker.

Reese yelled out, "Dad!" He and Karla went to his body and tried to hold him safe. Karla asked Reese if he was epileptic and Reese answered no. She watched as his eyes moving frantically from side to side.

Daniel B. Ayers, once again was having an out of body experience, seeing his son and daughter-in-law from above them on the ceiling, and now his pilot helplessly trying to figure out what was wrong.

He met his young mother in the upper atmosphere of the earth as they held each other's hands. Dan felt the love of his mother as she once more touched the cuticles of his fingers like she once did when he was an infant in her rocking chair.

The ascension slowed down and stopped, pausing for a brief still moment before the free fall, stopping, and then standing together on the grounds of the military cemetery where his father was buried in southwestern Milwaukee.

He watched as his mother smiled at him and let go of his hands as she turned to smoke and became absorbed into the earth below. Ashes to ashes, dust to dust. No words, just love, a sensation of duty completed.

Coming too with gasping breaths and opening his eyes, he was back in his mother's old room on the bathroom floor seeing the shocked look on everyone's face.

"Dad, are you okay?" Reese asked. Ace stood up, shakily to his feet, with Karla holding his arm to steady him. "Geez, dad, what the hell was that all about?"

"I'm okay, this has happened to me once before. It's hard to explain. I had another out-of-body experience caused by a strong emotional event. This time it was related to your grandma. Last time it had to do with Regina Putman's role in what happened to the country. My mom came to me in a dream as a young woman and she led me directly to this hair brush in her old room. She must have given it to that old woman or maybe the woman stole it from her. I'm not sure how to explain it, but that's it. She crossed over and is with Grandpa Ayer now.

"I understand, Ace." Karla reassured him that she believed every word.

Scott, Ace's personal pilot stood silently at the door, always on guard. "Can we go now, Sir? This place gives me the creeps."

"Thank you, Scott. Okay, I'm ready now. They all started walking back to the stairwell and then outside toward the waiting helicopter. Ace broke the silence. "Do you guy's mind if we just keep this all to ourselves?" They agreed and all stepped up into the chopper and made themselves ready for take-off.

****

Ailyn approached the make-shift landing zone in front of Hatty and Darin's bunker doors. She waited for the chopper to touch down and the engines to be killed before stooping over slightly and scurrying over to the now opening doorway. Steps unfolded mechanically to the ground and Ace stepped out with Karla and Reese. Scott stayed on board doing a final post-trip check-up so they would be ready to leave again when they were ready.

"We got a call while you were gone from John Pillsbury that you are needed tomorrow at his ranch. There is an urgent meeting scheduled with you and a guest that will arrive around one o'clock in the afternoon. We'll need to say our goodbyes and leave early in the morning."

"John didn't tell you what it was about?"

"No, just that it was urgent."

"Okay, let's make the most of the time we have left tonight then. Who knows when we will all be together again after this."

Ailyn didn't like the sound of that kind of talk coming from her clairvoyant husband, but she was dutifully obedient, understanding the responsibility of his new leadership role. "Penny, do you have the right ingredients on hand for us to make homemade biscuit dough from scratch?"

"Yeah, I think so."

"Let's have a fire and make biscuits on a stick."

"Mom, I couldn't tell you the last time I made those. That would be great," Hatty said with great excitement.

****

It was early evening. Darin and Reese had been tending to a nice sized campfire for a few hours. The pit had a solid bed of hot coals, perfect for turning the bread dough, rotisserie style on the end of the whittled branches. They each were picked special, approximately three quarters of an inch in thickness. Hatty was the most excited out of everyone there to start the roasting process. She took a cut out piece of the dough and began to work it between her hands into an elongated rope shape about nine inches long. Starting at the end of the stick, the dough was pressed carefully over the butt end and then candy caned down and around until she ran out of dough. Sealing up the creases carefully, welding the edges together, Hatty placed it over the hot coals and turned the stick slowly until the dough cooked to a golden brown perfection. The biscuit easily slid off the end, leaving a hole to be filled with her choice of sweet condiments, like peanut butter and honey and jams and jellies. Butter would be great but it was no longer available. They were messy and delicious.

"So, your dad and I are going to leave early in the morning. We're not sure when we will be able to come back. Promise me you all are going to be alright." Ailyn started to cry from the pent-up emotions. Reese and Karla had decided to stay behind this time and spend some quality time with Hatty and Darin and the girls. There were some building projects they needed extra hands with for the New Elmar Outpost. It had been several years since he and Hatty have been able to spend quality time together as brother and sister. Karla needed a different atmosphere to forget the past and move forward without constantly looking over her shoulders. Darin and the Rover crew built several small dome cabins for future travelers so they could have their own place and some privacy during their visits. Not exactly a honeymoon destination like the Virgin Islands, but it would do for now.

"Oh my God, I don't know where all those emotions came from. I love you all so much." The gushy response made for a sudden turn to uncomfortable laughter and everyone gave in to their emotions. It was another rare moment.

****

Day 652, May, 20th 2028
New Elmar, WI.

The helicopter blades started to turn and the twin turbo engines took control of the sound. Everyone had been together for breakfast. Now there would be more tears and hugs as the family reunion came to an abrupt close. The sounds produced from the chopper lessened and soon it was silent.

"I wonder what's going on that they needed to go to my mom and dad's?" Karla asked.

"I'm sure they will tell us when they come back again," Darin replied.

****

"Is he coming on his own, Ace?" asked John Pillsbury.

"I'm not sure. No one's heard from any of the Mrungs after the bombs."

"He said he has news to share with us. What time will he be arriving?"

"About one o'clock."

"Okay, that gives us some time to spend with you and Margaret. I'll take that tour now." Ace and Ailyn had landed on the Pillsbury helicopter pad shortly after eleven a.m. Margaret had them settled into their guest room on the sixth floor and they shared a small lunch together at noon. Ace felt very comfortable working with John and socially the two couples were equally matched.

****

Barren Mrung, stepped off the steps and ducked down out of habit. His extraordinary height caused Ace to look up slightly and as their hands met, they were poised upward on an uncomfortable angle.

"Hello Mr. Ayer, Mr. Pillsbury, I'm Barren Mrung. It's a pleasure meeting you both."

"Hi Barren, please feel free to call us Ace and John."

"Thank you, I appreciate that."

The three men stepped toward the bunker elevator and John pushed the number six button on the wall panel and soon they were stepping out and moving to the common area to sit comfortably and talk.

"Can I offer you a beverage, Barren?"

"A glass of that ice water would be refreshing, thank you."

"Ace?"

"Water is fine, John, thanks."

Barren began to tell the men some of what had transpired for him and his family over the last two years. After the grid failed, the entire Mrung family escaped the country together and flew to a secret private underground bunker deep underground in Iceland. They survived together as one family unit, relying on their own hard work and ingenuity. Former President Mrung spent his days with his family, spoiling his grandchildren with Marilyn. Barren explained that two weeks ago his father had passed peacefully in his sleep. "His last wishes whispered into my ear were for me to find the current leadership of the country and inform them of this news and to deliver these two envelopes into their hands." Barren gave Ace and John each an envelope and sat back silently offering them time to open and read the contents.

My Fellow Patriots,

Positions of leadership naturally come with tremendous responsibility. I don't have to tell you this, you already have accepted the duties and commitments your new position provides.

When I was President, I had the great privilege to pioneer and coordinate a world changing agenda. You're a part of that planning.

The evil powers that orchestrated the system end of the republic are mostly gone now.

So many souls were sacrificed needlessly from their malicious efforts.

The Middle East and China needed to manipulate a pawn in order to carry out their diabolical plans. That pawn was Regina Putman.

I've spent all my life amassing a sizeable fortune just to discover near the end of my day's that it doesn't mean a thing. The love of money is the root of all evil. I can attest.

After the failed assassination attempts on my life, I had a spiritual awakening of sorts. God himself helped me to come to terms with my wicked ways as a sinner and saved me from the horrible fires of hell.

Regina Putman is in hell right now, but not all of our enemies have joined her. Some accepted Christ in the last seconds. You'll see the truth someday.

Just know that everything happens for a reason and in God's time.

Some of those leaders of the many countries represented at the recent G-10 Summit were in on a divine plan to change the world.

The Federation means world peace and the elimination of poverty and famine. No longer will Money, power and greed be allowed to taint the minds of leaders representing the people of Earth.

Individuals like you were chosen to represent the people's voice and needs.

You will become responsible for enacting the changes that fulfill the Federation's succinct constitution.

The world will grow and be prosperous again. Great societies are built from a culmination of hard work and the rule of law.

Everyone has a purpose and specific skills and they simply desire fulfillment and happiness. Federation Earth will be the catalyst to accomplish this.

If threats develop, and they probably will, because men are flawed in this way by nature. They must swiftly be eliminated. I am sharing this in confidence with you because it directly affects our great country's existence which in turn effects our world. President Palarov must not be trusted. I realize he helped us when we needed to fight to survive the Chinese attack, but I am aware of his tortured mind. He speaks of agreement, but thinks of world domination. Let this letter be a serious warning not to fully trust his double speak and be ready to act when the time comes to neutralize Russia's threats. Knowing your enemies and keeping them close might buy you enough time to act first.

So, I leave you now in spirit and salute your unwavering commitment to serve mankind.

God Bless Federation Earth

President Ronald P. Mrung

John waited for Ace to finish reading and look up from the page of their identical letters. "I don't know what to say, Barren. Will you get involved politically like your father?"

"So, the grid collapse and the bombings turned out to be a silver lining which allowed my father's world vision to be enacted earlier than expected. I had plans to slowly get involved and maybe someday represent the country like he did. The chaos made it easier for his vision to be pushed forward and eliminate the threats to Earth's future."

John asked, "everyone's fully on board and in agreement except maybe Russia?"

"Yes."

Ace replied. "Your dad has always been six moves ahead on the chess board. I wish I would have had a chance to meet him in person."

Barren looked down and away, obvious to Ace that he missed his father very much and his heart was heavy. The Mrung family withstood a constant barrage of attacks while never giving up the fight to keep communism from taking over the country. The dark forces that unleashed brutal attacks on U.S. soil are all suffering the consequences of their own behavior. So many lives lost and sacrifices for the love of money. Never again will its power come ahead of the human race's survival.

****

Barren stayed until after dinner, allowing Margaret Pillsbury the honor of serving such a distinguished guest. Some additional details were discussed but mostly the rest of the evening was spent in enjoyment socially.

"You never really answered our question, Barren. How will you become involved with us in the future." Ace asked.

"I think our family has served long enough, Ace. We will live together as a family and try to catch up for lost time."

Ace nodded his head in approval. "I think that is a great idea, Barren. Your family has sacrificed enough. Please let John or I know if there is ever anything you need, okay?"

"Margaret, thank you so much for the delicious meal and hospitality. I believe if I leave right now, I can be home with my family before midnight to sleep in my own bed."

They saw Barren Mrung to the helicopter pad and waved as it turned northeast and accelerated out of site. Ace wondered if he would ever see the young man again.

CONSEQUENCES

Day 655, June 2, 2028

Moscow, Russia

Russian President Palarov was beyond inebriated, sitting back in his leather office chair, a near empty bottle of Beluga Noble Russian Vodka off center on the black ebony office desk. Only his personal assistant was near enough to hear his drunken babbling. All in Russian, speaking of lost opportunities and weakened ambitions as if he was carrying on a conversation with someone in the room.

Scratching the back of his head, he asked aloud. "Why would a country with the strongest military in the world bow down to a group of spineless infidels? I can't just sit by idly and let an opportunity like this pass us by, can I? We must act now while the rest of the world expects peace and is left unguarded like a ripe apple on a low hanging branch, ready for the picking. Take a bite of this apple. It's sweet and tart, but damn it all to hell it is so good. Yes!" Palarov yelled. "I will take what is rightfully mine for the love of Mother Russia. Payback for the years of oppression and never being taken seriously." The President passed out and lay back in his chair. Then his heart simply stopped beating.

****

Day 656, June 3, 2028
Norad Mountain, Montana

"Sir, I just heard from a contact in Russia that President Palarov is dead, alcohol poisoning."

Ace sat back, dumbfounded by the news. He recalled his recent conversation with Barren Mrung and the content of his father's letter. It seemed like a strange circumstance. Was it coincidental or could there have been malicious intent at play.

Not knowing the man personally, he wondered how Alphonsa would react to the news and thought he better be the person to tell him.

"Thank you, Mr. O'Neil. I need you to get Alphonsa Orlov on the radio for me, please."

"Yes, Sir. I'll try him right away."

Ace sat back and wondered the depths of emotional turmoil Palarov must have gotten to in his mind to drink himself to death. Or did he? Ace wondered if the Russian government would perform an autopsy on the body. Were nefarious actors involved in his death? That's the problem with not knowing all of the facts. Being left in the dark. Drawing one's own conclusions without all the facts. At least when we had reliable main stream media you could somewhat rely on their reporting and draw your own picture of what happened, even if that reporting was mostly fake news to fix an agenda.

"Sir, I have Alphonsa Orlov waiting on the radio."

"Thank you, Mr. O'Neil, I'll take it in here please. Alphonsa, have you heard any recent news yet about President Palarov?"

"No, I haven't, what's happened, Ace?" From the sound in his voice, he knew it was serious.

"Palarov is dead. Apparently from alcohol poisoning."

"Oh my, this is disturbing news. I know he did like his vodka, but not to this extreme."

"Was he struggling with anything emotionally that you were aware of Alphonsa?"

There was an uncomfortable pause on the air before Alphonsa replied. "He had his demons to deal with, Ace, just like you and I. He struggled dealing with the power that came with his role in leadership. Often, he would rely on others like myself to provide balance and direction. Does that help you at all?"

Ace could always count on Alphonsa to say the right thing at the right moments in their interactions with each other. A common trait among skilled chess players. "Well, I wanted to give you my sincere condolences, Alphonsa. I know you and he were well acquainted. Would you like to attend his funeral with me? I feel like I should go."

"I would welcome the chance to spend more quality time with you, my friend. We will attend together and I will act as interpreter for you and our group when needed. Let me know the arrangements and I will be ready."

"I will keep in touch after I learn the dates and times for the services. How are things going at your new outpost?"

"We have a few new guests that might consider staying permanently. It turns out they have some similar Russian ancestry and are quite familiar with the culture and their heritage. I'm trying to convince them to stay. One of them is a challenging chess player."

"That's great news, Al. I knew you'd make a great Governor. Thank you again, I'll be in touch, Norad Mountain, out."

Day 660, June 7th, 2028
Moscow, Russia

Ace and Alphonsa landed in Moscow and were greeted as dignitaries. A military escort preceded the motorcade of black Mercedes Benz limousines. It was a short distance to their hotel and Ace couldn't help noticing how clean the streets were. No broken windows or painted graffiti. The architecture was stunning. Each building was like a piece of ornamental antique artwork that has withstood the brutality of time. Built by the creative genius of craftsmen from yesteryear.

The motorcade pulled up to the front of the Radisson Royal Hotel. Important people have chosen to stay here because of the fantastic views and top notch security services.

The double doors of the limo opened on the entrance side of the hotel and Ace and Alphonsa stepped out under the covered awning. They were escorted through the spinning glass turnstile to the front lobby desk. The walls were covered with antique paintings that made it seem more like a museum than a hotel. The desk clerk greeted the two men by their full names in perfect English. They were given keys to their suites and were escorted along with their simple luggage to the glass elevators.

****

Ace and Alphonsa sat next to each other, off center, behind the front row at Palarov's memorial service which was held in the Cathedral of Christ the Saviour Church.

Both men were moved with emotion from the powerful rage of sounds of the majestic pipe organ. Palarov's body lay in open casket at the front of the open alter.

One of the procession members, a strikingly beautiful woman with long red hair turned around from the front row and glanced directly at Ace. It occurred with intention and gave him an uneasy feeling as the expression changed from solemn to a look of mystery. *Wow, that was uncomfortable. I wonder why she looked at me like that?* He decided to dismiss it, deciding the look must have been directed at someone else behind him.

****

At the cemetery, the same woman made direct eye contact with Ace. This time she stared for an uncomfortable length of time. Enough that it was awkward, making Ace look down and away to avoid her hazel-colored eyes shooting right through him. *What is up with this woman,* Ace thought.

They exited off the green Astroturf which sectioned off the memorial service from the rest of the cemetery grounds. Ace and Al walked toward their limousine and Ace caught her looking at him a third time from a short distance away. He asked Alphonsa. Pointing in her direction as she turned. "Do you know who the redheaded woman is right there, Al?"

"She was President Palarov's personal assistant, Veronika. Why do you ask Ace?"

"I've caught her looking awkwardly at me several times today."

"Maybe she blames you somehow for Palarov's death."

"Really, why would she think that?"

"Should we ask her?"

"Heck no, let's just let it go. It's probably nothing."

Ace and Al stepped into their limousine again and followed the motorcade procession out of the cemetery to the banquet hall where the attendees would be served a specially prepared meal and have opportunity to pay their final respects to President Palarov's family and friends.

****

With everyone seated at their table nearly finished eating, Ace excused himself from the table and made his way out into the hallway toward the hall's public bathroom area. He pushed on the golden handle of the door assuming it was the men's room and was followed inside by Veronika. She locked the door behind her and turned to look at him once more. His surprise was that he allowed her to muscle her way in behind him without any resistance.

She proceeded to check the four stalls for inhabitants. They were alone. "I need to speak with you alone Mr. Ayer."

"Okay, you have my full attention. What can I do for you?"

"I need you to know, this was inevitable. President Palarov was no longer compatible as a trusted leader of Russia. He was eliminated because of the threats he caused against the agenda built toward world peace, Mrung's agenda."

"Why are you telling me this now?"

"Because, I know you and Pillsbury both read the letter. You will be instrumental in fulfilling a plan that has been in action for over a century and no one will be allowed to act against it. Not anymore."

Ace had that look of confusion on his face, but knew enough not to ask any stupid questions. He decided to just shake his head in agreement and follow along instead of making waves.

Accepting this appropriate response, Veronika unlocked the door and peered outside carefully, then casually moved back into the main hallway as if she had just finished using the facilities.

Ace finished what he originally came to do and proceeded back to his table to join Al and the other seated guests.

Alphonsa could tell by the expression on his friend's face that he just had a peculiar experience. He whispered softly in a jokingly way, "did everything come out alright, Ace?"

"I'll tell you about it later." Alphonsa knew then that something actually did alarm his traveling partner.

****

The plane ride home was long and without further excitement. Both men took the liberty of catching up on lost rest from their travels. Ace thought about Veronika. She was a planted operative by President Mrung into the Palarov administration. *How could he have done that*, Ace wondered. Was she responsible in some way for Palarov's death? He didn't know if he was cut out for this type of political malfeasance. Accepting it was equal to becoming part of the actual act itself. *Will I ever see her again?*

As the plane was landing on the runway of the Dallas/ Fort Worth International Airport, Ace felt a strong pull toward questioning John Pillsbury, Elan Must, and President Baylor to determine their prior knowledge of President Mrung's planning. Just how the three men were actively part of the plan he couldn't tell, but the feeling turned into intuition and seldom was he proven wrong from such strong impressions. He would be flown back to John's ranch first, then planned on traveling with Ailyn to visit President Baylor next, ending with Elan at Norad Mountain. He needed answers before experiencing any future comfort serving in his new role.

"Thank you for traveling with me, Al."

"No, it was my pleasure, Ace, we make good travel partners. When can I expect a rematch in Minnesota?"

Ace knew he was referring to their chess playing hobby. "I'm not sure exactly. Ailyn and I will be taking a trip to go visit former President Baylor next, then I have some business to take care of at Norad Mountain. When that's completed, Ailyn and I would like to spend some more time with my family in Wisconsin. I think you'll be our next stop after that, so maybe in less than two weeks?"

"That sounds like a busy schedule, Ace. Make sure you stay balanced my friend."

"I will follow that advice, Al. Thank you."

The two men walked to Al's charter helicopter. Jet airline travel still wasn't operational up north. They shook hands and Al boarded the chopper and it took off shortly after. Ace had another strange feeling come over him. He closed his eyes and placed a black X over the vision that forced itself into his mind. The helicopter was crashed in a remote wooded area and was consumed by fire. He dismissed the image from his mind and verbally called it not to be so, a practice he had held onto all his life since his training in the mind control classes as a child. Many times, the parties involved would later mention close calls on the road in cars or near missed accidents that could have been deadly. The power of positive thinking is unexplainable. His belief was that Al, would be okay and the catastrophe would be diverted.

Entering his waiting Sikorsky helicopter, Ace buckled himself in and felt the vertical takeoff, then the pitch angle and the forward momentum as they gained speed traveling to the Pillsbury ranch helicopter pad. It took less then fifteen minutes and Scott, his personal pilot set them back down again.

Pressing the talk button on the entranceway's panel set off a soft alarm that notified and allowed the Pillsbury's to answer. They already knew they had guests though from the motion detectors located on their landing pad. John could see on the live monitor camera that it was Ace and his pilot. "Hi Ace, welcome back. Hit the second-floor button and come on down, we are working in our gardens."

"Okay, be right there, thanks." As the door opened, Ace realized he never took time before to tour the whole bunker. Other pressing issues always seemed to take up their time, like marrying off his son. The door opened to a huge underground food production factory. Smaller than Norad's but still very impressive. Every plant was brimming with fresh produce, obvious that John and Margaret were beneficiaries of the advanced hybrid seed technology. "Hi John, Margaret. It's nice to be back. Where's Ailyn?"

"She is in town with Zach, shopping for supplies to take up north to your family on your next trip."

"Excellent, before they get back, would you mind taking some time alone with me to review some things about my trip with Alphonsa?"

"Yeah, no problem. Honey, can I leave you for a little bit?" Margaret waved the two men off with her left hand from a few rows away. She was busy cultivating the rows by hand and knew it must be important.

"I need to check on something on the first floor with the air filtration system, we can talk on the way up."

"John, I don't know how else to ask you this other than directly. Did you have prior knowledge of President Mrung's plans before reading that letter?" Ace watched carefully for eye movements or other tells to determine John's truthfulness.

He paused and thought very carefully on how to answer. "Yes, Elan, and I all knew of Mrung's agenda and have worked to help him fulfill his plans."

"Did Baylor know too?"

There was no reason to try and hide anything further, John knew that Ace wouldn't be asking if he didn't already know the truth. "Yes."

Ace looked down and away. "Alright, now that I'm in on it, I can say that I'm not really happy being kept in the dark all this time. I think if I would have known earlier, I might not have so easily taken on the new role of leadership. Am I in any danger, or is any of my family in danger, which I don't have to remind you now includes Karla."

"No, Ace, it's not like that anymore." John saw Ace's facial expression was one of disbelief. "All of the threats to us or the Federation have been eliminated."

Ace interrupted, "yeah, that's what I'm talking about. While in Russia I met a woman named Veronika who was Palarov's assistant. I got the impression she was somehow responsible for the man's death and I learned it was all part of Mrung's plan."

"Okay, Ace, calm down. We can tell you everything, but before that happens, we needed to know if we could trust you completely to keep this information just between us. How about if the four of us meet and we bring you completely up to speed. This thing is bigger than all of us and honestly, we need you to help us follow through to make it happen."

Ace shook his head, somewhat in disbelief of what was happening. How the hell did he end up in such a peculiar position. "Okay, let's plan a meeting down by Baylor's in the Virgin Islands. I need to take a break and decompress from all of this espionage stuff. Ailyn and Margaret should come and they can keep themselves busy shopping while we meet."

THE CONSTITUTION

Day 666, June 13, 2028

St. Thomas, Virgin Islands

Traveling together after meeting at John's ranch, Elan, with his current single status, was going to be the odd man out once they all met up at the Baylor's. It was being disguised as a pleasure trip for the women's benefit, but the men were prepared to conduct business as usual when proper time allowed.

A personal driver was standing on the side of his shuttle van at the small airport holding a sign that read, 'Baylor party of five.'

They got onto the mini-bus and watched as the luggage was delivered to the vehicle and loaded into the underbody storage compartments by employees of the airport shuttle service.

Ace thought how different the reception was here in comparison to Russia. This seemed more fitting and it was less stressful.

They traveled along the jagged coastline of pure white sand beaches and vacation homes of every caliber. The residences became less frequent as the acreage between them increased along with building size and extravagance. The road took a sudden forty-five degree turn and the shuttle bus stopped in front of a black wrought iron gate with a guard house and two security officers who both approached the shuttle driver. They looked into the windows and subtly made eye contact with each passenger, then one moved back to the guard house to open the gate and the other waved them through. Ace looked back and saw the security guard pick up a phone and then place it back down again.

It took almost a mile of driving before arriving at the Baylor residence. Retiring from the position of President of the United States of America obviously had its perks. Ace raised his eyebrows to Ailyn showing his dismay. She commented. "Wow, what a beautiful home. Margaret, look at that view." The women were looking forward to spending some quality time together, doing the thing most women loved, shopping.

"Elan, have you been here before?" Ace asked.

"Three times, to deliver supplies and for other business."

"I can see why they chose this location. It seems secure and private. Does President Baylor still need all of his Secret Service protection?"

"We have less enemies to worry about now." Elan's comment was loaded with indirect intent that Ace fully understood. He couldn't wait to fully understand the unknown details. He'd know if they were holding back information from him. He was prepared to fight them for all of it.

The bus circled a lavish garden with flowing fountain statues of what looked like King Neptune and two mermaids. As it came to a stop, two bellmen approached and opened the shuttle cargo hold and began stacking the luggage onto wheeled carts. A personal assistant came to the doorway of the shuttle and greeted the new guests to the Baylor estate. She had a clipboard and copies of itinerarys that were passed out to each guest. Maggie exited the front doors of the mansion and waved calling out "hello," in an excited voice. "Welcome everyone! I'm so happy you came for a visit."

The women greeted her first with hugs and then Mitch Baylor came out the door and shook everyone's hands. "Welcome to our new place, you guys. It's a little elaborate for me and Maggie's taste, but Mrung told me I had no choice. We are enjoying retirement, if that's what it's called now. I haven't had more than a few days off since you guys took over. Let's all go inside and get you into your rooms. Roberta's given you itineraries to follow." He looked down at Margaret's and saw dinner was being served in two hours in the main dining room. "Let Roberta help you all to your rooms and Maggie and I will meet you for dinner at six o'clock. We'll eat first and then watch the sunset out on the back deck until bedtime. Business can wait until tomorrow. Okay, Ace?"

"That sounds great."

****

The group sat and enjoyed the evening sun setting across the ocean's flat horizon line. A slight breeze caused ripples of waves that broke onto the beach's edge.

Mitch and Maggie were great hosts, providing everyone with their favorite beverages as if it was planned in advance. Ace and Ailyn enjoyed tonic water with lime on ice, their go to when everyone else around them favored alcohol.

Small talk ensued as they all got to know each other more intimately as friends. Ace felt a strong compulsion to ask discreet relatable questions, but refrained, unsure of how it would affect the general mood of the evening. Patience was a character trait he had spent all his life in search of. The restraint of pen and tongue was difficult. Tomorrow would come soon enough.

He sat back in his chair and enjoyed listening to a conversation between Elan and Mitch about the day Elan presented the Rover to 'The House Appropriations Committee' for use by Space Force.

"After you were finished, the parties were split, like usual. I'll never forget what Mrung said to them, 'I wish you people would make up your minds, first you want everyone to have electric cars and hybrids, now you have a vehicle powered by the sun and because you didn't invent it you can't come to an agreement. Shit or get off the pot people!' Everyone laughed and it was then Ace realized just how influential President Mrung actually was. He knew in his heart that he was on the right side of history, but still questioned the ethical and moral sides of the recent Palarov situation.

Mitch yawned, and it became contagious. Everyone decided together they had enough for one day. Ace and Ailyn might never get used to all this time change traveling.

"Well, good night, everyone. See you at eight o'clock in the dining room. Sleep well."

****

Ace woke to the sunshine changing the illumination inside the plush guest room. It was just after six-fifteen and he got up and showered.

Ailyn followed him into the bathroom after hearing the water shut off. "This sure is a nice house."

"It's a mansion." Ace smiled at her and she took off her night shirt and threw it at him.

Stepping in and turning the water on, she peeked back out around the corner, "I still miss our house in Galesville."

"Yeah, it was a nice home, wasn't it." Changing the subject, "do you have anything specific you're looking for today while out shopping?"

"A few things for the kids. Some special clothes maybe for Hatty and Karla. I'll know when I see it."

"Well, I hope you have fun."

They walked together down to meet the other guests. All

of them except Elan were already in their seats. He was standing in front of what looked like an original copy of the Constitution hanging on the wall. Ace was tempted to ask if it was.

Mitch, asked him to come sit. There were several servants bringing bowls of food to the table to be served family style. Fruit, bakery options, scrambled eggs, bacon, ham and sausages, and pancakes. Hearty choices considering the world as they knew it today. Proof positive that status still paid dividends.

The three women left for town after breakfast was finished. The four men retreated back onto the open deck from last night. The morning sun was still in the eastern sky providing a cooler shade at the patio table.

A beverage cart was wheeled out and Mitch motioned with a slight nod to the staff understanding his body language without him actually saying, 'that will be all.'

"Can I offer any of you coffee?" Pouring himself a cup and plopping down a cube of sugar. He stirred it in and began to set it down at his chair spot.

"I'll take a cup, Mitch, thank you." Ace rarely turned down a good cup of coffee, he liked his black though.

"Ace, I understand you have a few questions?" Mitch set the hot cup down in front of him.

"Well, yes, I'll get right to the point. Has President Mrung been orchestrating all of this since coming down the escalator? Have all of you been involved with him from the start?"

"Yes, us and a small number of fellow patriots. Unfortunately, most of them have passed after the bombing, except for us and a few subordinate actors like Veronika who you met in Russia."

"Why me then? Why include me into your group when you did?"

"Well, that's a very good question too, Ace. Do you remember when you were active on Truth Social and you only posted written comments?"

"Yeah, I guess so, why?"

Elan interjected, "Do you realize how rare that quality is

these days, Ace? President Mrung had a psyops team analyzing posts from Truth Social's first launch day until the grid went down. There were only two other individuals in Truth Social's history that did this with you and now you are the only one of those three left. President Mrung was following your posts personally and even helped manipulate others to follow you for the benefit of his future plans."

"Was eliminating the Middle Eastern and the Asian countries all part of the original plan?"

"We didn't know this would happen until the opportunity became available, then we took advantage of it."

"John, was my daughter-in-law part of the psyops team?"

John answered directly looking Ace straight in the eyes. "She never was my daughter."

"What?" Ace got up from his chair and stood looking down at John Pillsbury.

"She's an undercover military operative meant to save and protect your son Reese from imminent danger."

"Wait, now that's a little out there. She's been acting the whole time? Your whole family has been acting?"

"Yes, none of us are actually related to each other." I'm a Lieutenant Colonel in Space Force.

Elan stepped in again. "Ace, Ronald Mrung was given a very unique opportunity only this small group of people are aware of. He was allowed to travel through time and learn about events that were to occur in the future. Knowing which events were beneficial for the preservation of mankind protected them from themselves and their actions, he was strategically chosen to receive this world changing information. We all have spent time together in the past and the future. I'm actually not from this time period. I was born in 1856, my real name is Nikola Tesla and I secretively invented time travel. Mrung's great-grandfather and I were best friends, he passed this secret onto his son and then he passed it onto Ronald's father and now it ends with Ronald P. Mrung himself, and us. We already know how you are going to answer our next question, Ace."

Mitch Baylor jumped in, "So, let me complete the picture for you Ace. Your family had been chosen to help carry out the Mrung agenda. He's gone now. We are all that's left. You are the newest founding member of a plan that has been in action for centuries and with Karla's and our help, you will pass this on to Reese and Hatty and Darin. Together we all will help save Earth from itself through the new Federation Earth agenda."

Elan sat back in his chair and placed his clasped hands behind his head. "Any other questions, Ace?"

"I don't know what to say, it all seems so far-fetched."

"Yeah, we knew you'd say that. It's all pre-determined."

Ace stayed standing, anxious and unsure of this new information he had just learned. He wanted to run, but his feet were kept in place. There was simply nowhere to go. "Okay, I'll do it," he said.

****

The alarm sounded and Ace's eyes opened to see the red digital numbers 3:33a.m, projected on the ceiling above him.

He was slightly out of breath as the dream he experienced was still vibrant inside his recall memory.

Ailyn woke up with him and they both got up and started their day's routine, coffee, shaving his bald head, then breakfast. As Ailyn was ready to go downstairs to work out, Ace mentioned, "Wow, did I ever have a doozy of a dream last night."

Ailyn put her fingers up onto Ace's lips and said, "tell me all about it tonight, I'm going to go work out."

The deja vu feeling rushed over Ace's entire body and mind. He knew he had been in that exact moment before in time and he shuttered from the awkward feeling.

"Love you, I'll see you later," Ailyn said reaching in for a kiss and then noticing her husband's facial expression and nervous body language.

"If anything happens today honey, I'll meet you here at the house."

THE END

Acknowledgement

Thank you once again to the team of individuals that have helped to make this trilogy series complete. Ann, Jenna, John and Jackie, and all the beta readers.

Thank you to Amazon, for providing authors with a useable,learnable, platform to self publish their books on.

Thank you to my Brother-in-law, Kevin, for helping to inspire the most important part of the story!

To all of the political leaders of the world, get your act together, okay! Quit allowing your egos and wallets to make decisions that affect your fellow citizens lives. Eventually you will reap what you sow and suffer the consequesnces of your own behaviors.

ABOUT THE AUTHOR

Dana B. Auer

Dana grew up the youngest of five boys on a rural hobby farm in eastern Wisconsin, where he learned basic skills of country living and survival passed down from a family history of hard work and living.
'3:33a.m,' is his debut novella.
'Enough Was Enough,' is the second book of a planned trilogy series.
'Federation Earth ,' is the third and final novella of the series.
A husband, and father, he now lives in Western Wisconsin.

BOOKS BY THIS AUTHOR

'3:33a.m'

Dan "Ace" Ayer, a sixty-four- year-old truck driver anticipating his retirement, has spent all his life preparing for unexpected disaster to keep himself and his family safe (if the worst happens).

But when terrorists attack, and the U.S Government
is comprimised, his fellow Americans become the
primary hurdle as they, too, fight for survival- the
powergrid goes down- the earth begins to shake,
and the air becomes unbreathable- acceptance
and self preservation lead to emotional turmoil as
so many of his friends and family are left behind.

'Enough Was Enough'

Dan "Ace" Ayer, has survived eight long months
in an underground bunker with his spouse, Ailyn,
and his friends, Mike and Sue. They question if the
long double winter has cleaned the air enough to
attempt to go outside. None of them know if anyone's
survived, but Ace's hope is strong, and he senses his
family has somehow made it through the devastation
that was maliciously unleashed on his beloved country.
Will the ground be able to grow plants? They have
prepared well, but an uncertain future awaits them.
The two couples have a plan. Only time will tell if they
will successfully feel the sun's warmth again.